FOOL'S GOLD ON CRUMCAREY

CRUMCAREY ISLAND - BOOK 4

BETH RAIN

Copyright © 2024 by Beth Rain

Fool's Gold on Crumcarey (Crumcarey Island: Book 4)

First Publication: 19th January, 2024

All rights reserved.

No part of this book may be reproduced in any form or by any electronic or mechanical means, including information storage and retrieval systems. Except for use in any review, the reproduction or utilization of this work, in whole or in part, in any form by any electronic, mechanical or other means now known or hereafter invented, is forbidden without the written permission of the publisher.

Published by Beth Rain. The author may be contacted by email on bethrainauthor@gmail.com

❋ Created with Vellum

CHAPTER 1

MOLLY

'Molly, when's the ferry due in?'

Molly jumped, dropped the napkin she was folding and whirled around, only to come face to face with her boss. Joyce Muir really did have the most amazing knack of appearing out of thin air – especially when she was least expected.

Patting her chest in a vain attempt to calm her racing heart, Molly narrowed her eyes.

'Why?' she said, her voice suddenly heavy with suspicion.

Joyce shifted from foot to foot, her eyes drifting aimlessly around the tired interior of the reception area. Staring at the bare plasterboard walls and bits of spray-foam insulation poking out from around the window was clearly preferable to making any kind of eye contact.

Molly frowned. Joyce was being... weird. Weirder

than usual, if such a thing was possible. After all, her boss was a bit odd at the best of times – vague, dithery and supremely forgetful. Right now though, she looked like she had ants in her pants... and that never boded well.

Biting her lip, Molly waited for Joyce to answer in her own time. She'd learned the hard way that any attempt to hurry her usually ended in disaster. Still, she couldn't quite contain her sigh of frustration when Joyce started to fiddle with a pile of out-of-date calendars that had been set aside for recycling. She piled them up, neatened the corners, and then fanned them out along the old trestle table Molly used as a front desk. Then she turned and grabbed a half-moulted feather duster from a shelf and started to waft it around.

'You okay?' said Molly at last, unable to keep a hint of concern out of her voice.

'Fine, fine,' muttered Joyce. 'But... the ferry?'

'It's due in about three-quarters of an hour, I think,' said Molly, glancing at the ancient carriage clock above the door. The old thing looked decidedly out of place against the un-decorated plasterboard – and it didn't really serve any purpose considering Joyce always forgot to wind it. Molly would gladly do it herself, but for some reason, her boss wouldn't let her anywhere near it. 'Why *exactly* are you asking about the ferry? Are you going somewhere?'

It wouldn't be the first time Joyce had arranged a

little holiday for herself and forgotten to tell Molly anything about it until she was - quite literally - on her way to the ferry port. Considering Molly was the one and only member of staff at the Crumcarey Conference Centre – that sort of thing was *never* a good surprise!

'Oh... no,' said Joyce. 'I'm not going anywhere... and no reason, really,' she added, plonking the duster down on top of the clean napkins Molly had been busy folding just to give herself something to do.

'Are you sure?' said Molly, her tone still heavy with suspicion.

'Quite sure,' said Joyce. 'Oh... that's right... I *knew* I had something to tell you. We've got some guests booked in.'

'Guests?' said Molly. 'That's great!'

They hadn't had anyone to stay at the conference centre since well before Christmas. Actually – come to think of it, they'd barely seen anyone since the wine festival.

The problem was – the place was in a total state. It was barely fit for human habitation... so this news of guests was a bit of a mixed blessing. On the one hand, they were desperate for customers, but on the other... the place might fall down around their ears while they were sleeping.

Things at the Crumcarey Conference Centre were dire. Worse than dire. In fact, if there was even the slightest sniff of another full-time job available on the island, Molly would be down on her knees begging for it right about now. There was no chance of that though. So, Molly was left to worry and daydream in equal measure - while doing her best to stop the place from falling apart completely while Joyce turned a blind eye.

'Yes, it *is* great, isn't it?' said Joyce, blithely unaware of Molly's less than cheerful train of thought.

'So… how many, and when are they coming?' said Molly.

'Now!' said Joyce, frowning at her. 'They're on the ferry.'

'The ferry?!' squeaked Molly, her eyes growing wide. 'This morning's ferry? The one that's turning up in less than an hour?'

'Yes!' tutted Joyce. 'Goodness, girl – keep up! I'm sure I wrote it all down in the diary. You really need to keep on top of these things!'

'The diary?' breathed Molly, feeling like she was slowly but surely losing the plot. Would that be the mythical diary that hadn't been seen since the wine festival? The one that had seemingly disappeared onto another plane of entropy.

Useful. Very useful.

Molly shook her head. Going into panic-mode wasn't going to help anyone right now, was it?!

'How many guests are we expecting?' she asked again, more than aware that her voice had risen into a stressed-out, quivering falsetto.

'Oh… just nine,' said Joyce, unwrapping one of the Christmas chocolates that were still sitting, untouched, in their glass bowl and popping it into her mouth.

'Nine?!' gasped Molly, her heart rate going into overdrive.

People always said that life here on Crumcarey was idyllic – serene and relaxed. Clearly "people" didn't have to work for Joyce Muir.

Molly took a deep breath. She only had forty-five minutes - she didn't have the luxury of going into a tailspin! What she needed right now was to get her head on straight and work this out.

The conference centre consisted of one ancient, crumbling castle, and a bunch of decrepit portacabins. The castle *could* be turned into something really special - but in reality, the place needed a fortune spending on it – and Joyce *really* didn't have one of those lying around! As it was, just a tiny portion of the old building had received any kind of attention over the years… and it showed!

Molly adored the old castle… at least, the bits of it that hadn't been hidden under a bunch of half-arsed plasterboard like the reception! If she was being honest though, the portacabins weren't fit for much other than a can of petrol in the middle of the night… and a lit match or two. That was one of her dearest fantasies when Joyce became unbearable!

Molly wrinkled her nose. She hated having to show guests to their rooms in the "luxury executive accommodation" – as Joyce called the cabins on the website. It was embarrassing – especially when they got to the communal toilet and shower block that was little more than a couple of old caravans bolted together. The floor in there always felt like it was just about to give way. How they hadn't lost a guest through it yet was anyone's guess.

Still – nine guests meant that every single bed in the place would have to be pressed into action. They'd been so quiet over the past year that Molly only kept one room made up and ready - just in case of any random walk-ins. It hadn't happened for longer than she could remember… but at least keeping that space clean and aired made her feel like she was doing something useful.

As for the other rooms – the ones out in the portacabins – there simply wasn't any point. The bedding would just get damp and dusty and then need changing every week for no good reason.

Unfortunately, that meant she had her work cut out for her if she was going to be anywhere near ready in time to greet the new arrivals.

'Right – we'd better be quick,' she said. 'We need to get all the rooms sorted out.' She just hoped the bedding didn't smell too damp after its long confinement in the large blanket boxes.

Joyce shrugged and nibbled on a second chocolate. Molly stared at her. She clearly didn't care in the

FOOL'S GOLD ON CRUMCAREY

slightest that this was the biggest booking they'd had in... forever.

'They're just a bunch of archaeologists,' said Joyce, rolling her eyes. 'It's not like they're going to be expecting much in the way of creature comforts, is it?'

Molly bit her tongue to stop herself from saying anything stupid. It would be just as well if the poor blighters weren't expecting too much... because they certainly weren't in for a comfortable stay. If it was up to her...

No point going down that road, Moll!

It *wasn't* up to her. There wasn't any point wasting any more time and energy on daydreams that would never come true - it only put her in a bad mood. She just hated the fact that there was so much potential in this place - but Joyce simply didn't seem to care.

'I bet they're used to staying in tents,' said Joyce. 'The cabins will be a spot of luxury for them after that... I mean, at least they won't get blown away!'

'Right,' muttered Molly. 'Anyway - I'd better get this sorted... are you collecting them from the ferry?'

'Nope!' laughed Joyce. 'That's what I pay you for! Anyway - I've got something important to do...'

Molly stared at her boss. Was she really expecting her to do this on her own in just forty-five minutes? Forty minutes. Half an hour. Whatever - she *had* to be kidding!

'Here's the list of names,' said Joyce, yanking a

crumpled bit of brown paper from her back pocket and waving it at her.

Molly grabbed it before she had the chance to lose it.

'Good, that's everything you need,' said Joyce. 'See ya!'

Molly hadn't even managed to smooth the creases out of the scrap of paper before Joyce disappeared outside, leaving the door banging behind her.

'I'm lucky to have this job, I'm lucky to have this job!' Molly chanted like a mantra, willing herself to believe the words.

It was *fine* – she'd just have to deal with this on her own. Just like she always dealt with the wine festival on her own. She could do this. In fact – *not* having Joyce's "help" would probably make things easier.

Scanning the list of names in front of her, Molly did her best to make out Joyce's untidy scrawl. The list started with *Professor Geoffrey Estwick* and ran all the way down to *To Be Confirmed.* Right. So – eight people – and *maybe* nine. She'd better get on with it!

Molly turned to the large blanket box that sat behind the desk, flipped open the lid and started counting out pillowcases, all the while wondering what a bunch of archaeologists were planning to do on Crumcarey.

Wouldn't it be great if they were coming to do a survey of the castle?!

That would be a dream come true. The place

certainly needed a whole heap of money spending on it… preferably before it fell down!

Molly had broached the subject a couple of times with Joyce over the years. She'd even offered to research if there were any grants available to fix up the roof. Sadly - Joyce had approached the plan with the same enthusiasm she applied to running her business - she just ignored it!

'Maybe I was wrong,' murmured Molly, straightening up and heading for the door that led out towards the cabins.

Maybe Joyce had actually started the ball rolling… but also… maybe not. Molly didn't want to get her hopes up only to be disappointed. As usual.

'Well, I guess I'll find out soon enough!'

CHAPTER 2

TIM

Tim wrapped his fingers around the takeaway cup and yawned widely. The wind was getting up, and he was glad of the comforting warmth as it seeped through his gloves. He'd asked for the largest coffee available, and was planning to make it last as long as humanly possible!

Staring around the grey, windy harbour in the half-light, Tim watched in amusement as his classmates tucked into their sandwiches with gusto.

'You'll regret it!' he muttered into the fragrant steam wafting up to greet him.

Something told him the ferry trip over to Crumcarey was going to be anything *but* smooth sailing. Not that it bothered him in the slightest. Tim had only had a very light breakfast about an hour ago – unlike the rest of the first-year archaeology students, who'd all wolfed down full Scottish breakfasts – complete with fried haggis and goodness knows what else. Now here they were, adding extra sandwiches on top. It was a recipe for disaster!

Tim knew how rough these crossings could get – after all, he'd spent his entire childhood travelling around on the big old ferries that serviced the Scottish islands, linking them to the mainland. In fact, he still called the island of Brumeldsay his home – even if he was currently living in student accommodation on the mainland.

Tim might be used to island life… but he'd never been to Crumcarey before. If it had been up to him - he wouldn't be heading there now, either. All first-year students on his course had to do some kind of fieldwork, but this little jaunt didn't really float his boat.

For one thing, the whole point of going to university was to experience something *other* than life on a tiny Scottish Island. He already had twenty-five years' experience of that under his belt! For another thing, the professor in charge didn't like Tim one little bit. Maybe it was something to do with him being a mature student.

Tim hated being called that – especially as he was only a handful of years older than his classmates. That said, sometimes it felt like he was centuries older – and not just because he knew how to cook a pan of rice and use a washing machine.

After putting his plans on hold to nurse his mother through two bouts of cancer and the full-on treatments that had saved her life – Tim felt ancient compared to the others. They were a nice enough bunch – just a little bit wide-eyed and naïve. Plus, they had a habit of swallowing everything their professors told them without questioning a single thing.

Come to think of it, that was probably the professor's problem with him. Tim questioned everything he was told – and that made him a bit of a thorn in the side of Professor Geoffrey Estwick!

Take this trip to study Crumcarey's standing stones for instance. There was just something... *odd* about them. Obviously, Tim had never seen them in real life, but something was telling him they were off on a wild goose chase!

'Come on, everyone, look lively!' called the professor from the front of the queue as the ferry started to swing around in a great arc, cutting through the water as it neared the harbour wall.

Tim shook his head. There was precisely no reason to *look lively* just yet. It would take a good twenty minutes for the cars to leave the boat. Then any cargo would be loaded before the crew was ready for the foot passengers to board.

'Come on, Tim - don't hold us up!' grumbled the professor.

Tim rolled his eyes as all the other students excitedly snapped lids onto their empty sandwich boxes and joined the professor at the front of the queue like eager primary school kids.

Straightening up and taking another sip of his coffee, Tim ambled over to the others. There wasn't any point winding the professor up before they'd even got there. It was bad enough that the grumpy git knew he didn't really want to be there in the first place.

'Now then,' said the professor, pulling a familiar book from the inner pocket of his stinky waxed-cotton jacket, and cracking it open at a page that was marked with a bright orange post-it note. 'Have you all read the chapter I emailed you?'

There was a general murmur of assent from the group. Tim just nodded. He'd read it – adding in the massive pinch of mental salt it deserved as he went. Professor Estwick didn't seem to realise that the old Crumcarey guidebook was a running joke - both on Crumcarey *and* Brumeldsay. Mainly because the photographs in the book were all taken on Brumeldsay - *not* Crumcarey. And the words? Well... they were a cobbled-together cocktail. Descriptions of Brumeldsay were sprinkled liberally with place-names from Crumcarey... and then topped off with pure fiction.

Tim had made the mistake of trying to draw the professor's attention to this... and had received a failed essay to return the favour. Professor Estwick was having none of it. According to him, Crumcarey's stone circle was an unexplored treasure - an archaeologist's dream come true.

'See here,' said the professor, raising his voice over the

wind, which seemed to be building by the second. 'This could well be the altar stone. This is where we'll concentrate our initial investigations - and we'll work methodically outwards from there.' He puffed out his chest, pulling himself up excitedly. 'I don't need to tell you again that these standing stones are impressive, undocumented, and could be a unique example of an early settlement.'

Tim sighed and rolled his eyes.

'Problem, Mr Stewart?' he snapped.

Tim had to force himself not to roll his eyes again.

'Nope - just excited to get going!' he said, smiling at the professor. It was as much as he could do not to giggle as the old git visibly bristled. He *definitely* didn't like him!

Ah well… it didn't really bother Tim. Just like being drafted in as a last-minute replacement for one of the other students didn't *really* bother him. As much as he'd prefer to be off exploring somewhere that wasn't a dodgy stone circle on a remote Scottish island, it had to be better than being stuck inside the stuffy lecture theatres back at the university.

Tim liked nothing better than being outside. That's why he'd chosen archaeology when he'd been too late to get onto the geology course. That's what he'd really wanted to study, and if it had been down to him, he'd have waited another year. But his mum had been desperate to see him begin his own adventure – and Tim would do practically *anything* for his mum. Seeing her happy meant more to him than anything else in the world.

Of course, she thought it was hilarious that he'd been roped in to go to Crumcarey, and had sent him her own copy of the guidebook in the post as a joke.

Why the university had agreed to a field trip right in the middle of winter was beyond both of them, though. Sure, signs of early spring might be appearing down south, but up here, north of north Scotland... things were a very different story. Sunrise was late, sunset was early, and the light levels in between were... questionable. Especially when the storm clouds piled high and soaked the islands.

Tim just prayed that the weather gods would be on their side this week... otherwise, they could all end up stuck in their accommodation. He'd raised this point with the professor when the trip had been announced but had been loudly shouted down. In fact - he'd been told if he couldn't handle a bit of weather, he was on the wrong course. Tim had shrugged and kept his mouth shut after that. There wasn't any point trying to explain that there were days you couldn't physically stand up because of the wind - let alone conduct an archaeological survey.

Tim wasn't worried for himself – he'd experienced plenty of storms in his life. He wasn't sure how the others would fare, though. He quickly cast his eyes over his classmates and sighed. Yep - they were going to get very cold and very wet – even if the weather behaved itself. They'd all been told to bring appropriate clothing – but most of them were already shivering in the early morning breeze. They were all wearing thin anoraks, and an array of hand-knitted sweaters, ripped jeans and patchwork dungarees.

'When we get there, we'll take the rest of the day to get settled into our accommodation,' said the professor. 'Then we can head over to the stones bright and early tomorrow.'

Tim stared hard at his shoes so that he didn't catch the professor's eye again. The university was shelling out for them all to stay at the Crumcarey Conference Centre. On paper - it sounded great… and even the website made it look halfway decent. But the place had a reputation. The word p*rimitive* was used a bit too often for his liking. With any luck, the rumours were out of date. Maybe it had been improved and modernised. Maybe…

'Right… let's get going!' said the professor, beckoning for them all to follow him down the ramp onto the boat. Tim brought up the rear with an impending sense of doom.

This whole trip was a joke, wasn't it?!

The real question was how the professor had managed to secure funding when all he had to go on was the old guidebook and a couple of photos his own mother had snapped of the standing stones when she'd visited about three years ago.

Even though the prof's dear old mama had clearly

been pissed as a fart when she'd taken them, anyone with a pair of eyes could see that the stones in the wonky, blurry photographs didn't remotely resemble the ones in the guidebook. And for good reason. The guidebook actually showed the Ring of Brumeldsay.

'You excited?' said the girl in front of Tim, turning back to grin at him with shining eyes beneath her blue fringe and crochet beanie.

'Can't wait!' said Tim, returning her smile. She was going to be one of the first to freeze!

CHAPTER 3

MOLLY

Wrinkling her nose, Molly glanced around the cramped reception. A bunch of damp, dishevelled students and one very disgruntled-looking professor stared back at her.

The last person through the door had left it open, and it was banging in its frame with every gust of wind - making a right old racket. Molly knew she should edge her way through the crowd to shut it properly before one of the rusty hinges gave up the ghost... but if she was being honest, she didn't want to get any closer to them than she had to. Not only were her new arrivals soaked to the skin, but there was also a faint waft of sick coming from the group.

The drive back from the ferry port had been practically unbearable. Molly had arrived ten minutes late – frantic, frazzled and a little out of breath - only to find all but one of her guests standing around in the rain.

That one had had the sense to find shelter… but worryingly, it hadn't been the professor!

The minute Molly had bundled them all into the minibus, she regretted not putting her foot down and insisting that Joyce should be the one to pick them up. The scent of unwashed student combined with a heavy hit of seasickness had been enough to make her eyes water, and she'd been forced to keep her window cracked open all the way back, even though the weather was throwing a hissy fit.

Now that she had them there, Molly was desperate to allocate their grotty rooms so that they could all have a wash… or at the very least, get changed!

'Could… erm… could one of you close the door, please?' she called over the din, doing her best to sound as polite as possible instead of mildly annoyed… and slightly nauseous.

Someone at the back of the group gave her the thumbs up and jostled past the others to give the heavy door a slam against the wind. The noise level instantly dropped by a couple of decibels, and Molly breathed a sigh of relief.

'Thank you!' she said, noting that it was the one relatively dry student who'd come to her aid. She'd noticed him on the minibus too. Whenever she'd peeped in the rear-view mirror, there had been a small smile playing on his lips – the only part of his face that had been visible under a warm hat that he wore pulled down low over his ears.

'No probs!' he said, as that same smile beamed in her direction. He still hadn't taken his hat off... though that was probably a good thing considering they'd all be traipsing back out into the wind and rain as soon as she'd answered any questions and gathered the room keys together.

Molly took a deep breath and prepared herself for a whole lot of grumbling. The rest of them were throwing morose looks around the cramped reception, and it was obvious they weren't particularly impressed.

Just wait until you see where you have to sleep!

Molly had a feeling she was going to have her work cut out with this lot. It looked very much like she'd been landed with a bunch of wide-eyed teenagers away from home for the first time. Not only were they drenched from head to toe, but their crammed rucksacks were soaked too. From the muttered complaints she'd caught on the ride back to the conference centre, it sounded like they'd all left their bags out on the deck of the ferry for the entire journey.

'Any questions before I show you to your rooms?' said Molly, sweeping the keys into an old plastic ice cream tub and grabbing the crumpled list of names from the desk. She hadn't had a chance to match up the names with the rooms before she'd had to rush off to collect them... so her plan was to work from the top down. The professor had already proved himself to be a rude, pompous pain in the bum, so he certainly wasn't getting any kind of preferential treatment!

'I've got a question?' said a girl with a sodden blue fringe peeping out from underneath a hat that looked like it needed to be wrung out. She was holding an expensive-looking mobile phone in the air and was waving it around - clearly trying to get some reception.

'Yes?' said Molly, trying to keep a straight face even though she knew what was coming.

'Where's the best reception here?'

Molly resisted the urge to laugh as the others all sat up – suddenly paying attention and looking like a bunch of eager meerkats. The truth was, there *wasn't* any reception here - they were well out of reach of the nearest mast.

'The whole conference centre is a bit of a black hole, I'm afraid,' she said. 'There's a pay phone in the corridor between the cabins… but it's out of order. If there's an emergency, we've got a landline in here.'

A loud groan came from the group, and it was as much as Molly could do to stop herself from rolling her eyes.

'You might find pockets of signal here and there around the island, but it's pretty rare!' she added cheerfully.

The entire group seemed to deflate - apart from the guy who'd closed the door for her – who she quickly dubbed "laughing-boy" in her head. Going by the smile that was still tugging at the corner of his mouth, he was finding the whole thing hilarious.

Molly lowered her eyes to her list for a moment,

wondering which one he was. He didn't look quite as bewildered as the rest of them nor as bedraggled. He was wearing a pair of ancient-looking walking boots and well-worn waterproofs. There was no telling which one he was, though. Shame… if she was tempted to give anyone preferential treatment right now – he'd be the guy on the receiving end!

'Right…' she sighed, 'let's head back out. I'm sure you all want to settle in!'

Molly waited for them all to make their way back out into the rain and then brought up the rear.

'Thanks!' she said in surprise as she ducked outside only to find the same guy holding the door open for her so that it didn't crash around in the wind.

He nodded at her, his smile widening into a grin. Hmm… there was something in that smile that hinted at trouble.

'Can we get on with it?!' demanded the professor.

Molly nodded and made a dash for the first – and worst – of the portacabins. The professor had just sealed his own fate. He was right at the top of her list and frankly, the sooner she dropped him off the better!

'That's the shower block there,' she called over her shoulder, pointing at the bolted-together caravans.

'Well, we don't need a guided tour of that, idiot girl!' grumbled the professor, holding on to his hat with one hand as the wind caught at the front of his jacket, making him look like a grumpy crow. 'Show us to our rooms before we drown!'

'Very well, follow me,' she muttered.

This should take the pompous ass down a peg or two.

'Mr Estwick?' she said lightly, turning the handle of the first cabin, then giving the door a good kick when it refused to open.

'Professor!' he huffed.

'Right. You,' said Molly. 'This is your room.'

Molly stepped up into the little corridor, wincing as the floor sagged slightly under her weight. She pushed open another door to her right, revealing a tiny single bedroom. She'd done her best to air it by leaving the window cracked open - but it hadn't really helped. The room still smelled old and fusty - and thanks to the vicious wind whistling through the tiny gap, it was seriously chilly.

'This can't be right,' muttered the professor, sticking his head around the corner and then withdrawing it so fast it was a miracle he didn't get whiplash.

'This is you,' said Molly with forced politeness. 'I thought you'd prefer a room to yourself – and all the others are shared.'

And I want to get rid of you first!

The thought popped into her head, but Molly just about managed to bite her tongue in time to stop it from slipping out.

As the professor peeped around the corner again, Molly caught sight of the others watching from the doorway. Laughing Boy seemed to be having trouble keeping his giggles in check because his shoulders were definitely shaking underneath his wet weather gear.

'But...?' said the professor. 'But surely...?'

He glanced over his shoulder at the students all watching from the main doorway. Molly got the distinct impression he wanted to ask if she had anything nicer available - but wasn't comfortable doing so while the others were within earshot.

'Fine!' he sighed, his shoulders slumping in defeat. He pushed past her and dumped his damp duffel bag onto the bed, wrinkling his nose at the sight of the thin cover with its swirly orange pattern straight out of the 1970s.

'Great!' said Molly with a forced smile, handing him a key from the ice cream tub. 'I'll leave you to make yourself... erm... comfortable!'

Heading back into the little hallway, Molly opened the door opposite the professor's room. This one was a twin. She glanced down at her crumpled list and then out at the students.

For a brief moment, she locked eyes with Laughing Boy and felt an insane urge to giggle. Hmm... she'd changed her mind. Sod preferential treatment... she needed to get him ticked off her list asap - before he got her into trouble! It was hard enough to appear professional in a place like this - without having someone tempting you into a laughing fit left, right and centre!

'Right!' she said, doing her best to pull herself together. 'Ben and Rhodri - this is you.'

Two lanky-looking teenagers clambered into the portacabin and mooched past her. They looked anything but pleased – and Molly wasn't sure if it was because of the grotty room she'd just given them, or the fact they had to sleep in the same cabin as Professor Grumpy-Pants.

'I'll leave you to settle in,' she said, before hurrying back out into the rain and beckoning for the remaining six students to follow her.

Molly worked her way down the list as quickly as she could, dropping the three girls off in a shared room, and then turning to the three remaining guys. Two of them were looking decidedly stroppy by this point, but the third still had his signature grin going on under the brim of his hat.

Well... this would decide it...

'Noah and Jan?' she said.

Stroppy boys number one and two stepped forward and climbed up into the remaining portacabin with very poor grace.

Great. That left her alone with the smile that spelled trouble, then!

'To Be Confirmed?' said Molly, raising an eyebrow.

'That's me! Tim Stewart,' he said, his smile growing broader as he offered her his hand.

Instead of taking it, Molly took a tiny step backwards and pretended to ignore his outstretched fingers. Somehow, she didn't think it would be a good idea to make physical contact with this guy. That smile of his was already doing something funny to her, and she didn't need to add any other complications to the mix!

'Come this way!' she said, doing her best to sound as stern as possible… mainly in an attempt to stop him from picking up on the fact that he'd managed to turn her into a breathless idiot.

CHAPTER 4

TIM

Tim followed Molly back through the cabins with growing trepidation. By this point in proceedings, he was finding it impossible not to be at least *mildly* alarmed. So far, the rooms had all been similar… similarly *awful*, that was!

Actually… the professor's had been even worse than the others. Tim would bet anything that Molly had chosen the grimmest of the lot just for him… but then, he *did* deserve it. The old git had been decidedly unpleasant to her. In fact, he didn't seem to like her at all for some reason.

Tim couldn't understand it. Molly was… unexpected… and he was having a hard time keeping his eyes off her. What on earth was someone quite so lovely doing in a dump like this?

'Keep up!' she huffed ahead of him.

Tim grinned. Her prickliness didn't fool him for a

second. He'd seen her bite back a smile more than once already. In fact, he'd just spent the last twenty minutes playing a little game which involved catching her eye as frequently as possible (one point) and coaxing a smile out of her (ten points). It had been a fun distraction from having to focus too hard on this awful place – and he was on forty-seven points and counting!

It hadn't taken Tim long to realise he probably wasn't even on Molly's list - he'd been such a late addition to the party. Now he was wondering if she had a room for him at all, or if he was going to have to kip under the trestle table in the draughty reception!

Ah well, he'd stayed in some pretty dodgy places over the years. It didn't really matter - it was only for a week. Besides, he had a sleeping bag tucked into the bottom of his backpack. It was small but mighty - so at least he'd be warm, no matter what hole Molly was preparing to stick him in!

'Where are we going?' he laughed as Molly led him away from the cabins back towards the crumbling castle.

'You'll see,' she said, not slowing her pace or even looking at him.

Tim grinned at her back and then stared up at the old building. It really was quite impressive - even if it did need some serious TLC.

Oh boy, this was going to be a whole heap of fun… why did he get the feeling Molly was about to bung him in the dungeon? He shrugged. It didn't matter to him as long as he had somewhere to sleep.

Tim had a superpower - and that was the uncanny knack of being able to sleep practically anywhere. It had served him well while he'd been caring for his mum. One night, he'd drifted off on her bedroom floor with his head propped up on one hand. He'd woken up several hours later with the worst case of pins and needles of his life. Still - it had been worth it to see the amusement in his mum's eyes as he'd danced around her room, trying to get the feeling back in his hand.

'So... how long have you worked here?' he said, deciding that he might as well grab the opportunity to find out a bit more about Molly.

'Too long,' she sighed, before coming to an abrupt halt and clapping her hand over her mouth. She shot an accusing glance at him, as though he'd just forced the words out of her.

Tim smirked. Molly widened her eyes and then shook her head, her hand still over her mouth.

'Don't worry,' he said. 'I won't tell anyone.'

'Good,' she mumbled through her fingers, her voice only just audible over the wind. 'Erm... thanks,'.

'Okay... different question,' he said. 'How long have you lived here?'

'Forever,' said Molly.

'Cool,' said Tim. She clearly wasn't in the mood for conversation.

'Come on, let's get inside!' she said, hurrying

towards the reception door as if it was home-base in a game of catch.

Tim followed her into the undecorated plasterboard box that was so at odds with the castle's ancient exterior and pulled the door closed behind him. Pausing to catch his breath now that the wind wasn't shoving rain straight into his face, Tim grabbed the straps of his rucksack and hoisted it more securely onto his shoulders.

'Sorry to make you carry that all over the place!' said Molly as she tossed the plastic tub and crumpled list she'd been carrying onto her desk.

'It's fine!' he said with a shrug, glad to find that she was smiling at him, though she didn't seem to want to meet his eye for some reason.

Quick, say something to make her feel more relaxed.

'You know… I wasn't even meant to be on this trip,' he said. 'I didn't want to come.'

Molly's eyebrows shot up and Tim instantly wanted to kick himself. Instead of making things better, he'd just inadvertently managed to offend her by suggesting he hadn't wanted to visit Crumcarey - the island that had been her home for her entire life!

'Sorry,' he said quickly. 'It's not because I didn't want to see Crumcarey! What I meant was… I didn't want to be on this course at all. I wanted to study geology but I applied too late to get a place - so I got landed with Professor Git-face instead.'

Molly's eyes widened in surprise and Tim shut his

mouth. This was going from bad to worse. There was something about this beautiful woman that seemed to have given him verbal diarrhoea! It was so weird… normally, he didn't give two hoots what people thought of him. They could take him or leave him and it didn't bother him in the slightest. Just a few minutes alone in Molly's company, however, and he was desperate for her to like him.

"Mature" student, my arse!

'Anyway,' he said 'I come from an island just like Crumcarey. I mean… if your guidebook is anything to go by, it really is *just like it.*'

'Huh?' said Molly, crinkling her nose.

'Brumeldsay?' said Tim quickly. 'That's where I grew up.'

'Oh,' said Molly. 'Never heard of it.'

'It's where all the photos in the Crumcarey guidebook were taken.'

'Oh,' she said again.

'You know, I thought there would be more trees here!' he said. One last joke. One last-gasp attempt to make her laugh.

'Everyone says that,' sighed Molly, turning to grab the last key from a line of hooks behind the desk.

Tim let out a long sigh and promptly decided he'd be doing himself a favour if he kept the jokes to himself from now on. Something told him that Molly was going to be a hard nut to crack.

'See that door over there,' she said pointing to the

wall behind him. 'That one leads to the Dining Hall – that's where you need to go for breakfast tomorrow.'

Tim nodded.

'Come on then,' she said. 'I'll take you up to your room.'

'Up?' said Tim. 'Not going to lock me in the dungeons then?'

Maybe she was going to lock him up in the tower and have her wicked way with him instead!

In your dreams, Tim Stewart!

This woman was quickly turning him into an idiot. The sooner he was in his room, the better.

'Lead the way,' he said, preparing himself for the worst. The room couldn't be any worse than the dodgy portacabins... could it?! Even if it was an undecorated box made out of badly joined-up plasterboard like the reception, at least it wouldn't rock around in the wind!

Molly headed for a door that was tucked in behind the desk. She gave it a hefty kick and shoved it open.

'Mind your head,' she said as she beckoned for him to follow her. 'The old stone is really low through here.'

Tim ducked low and followed her through the gap. When he straightened back up, he felt like he'd just stepped through a portal back in time.

'Wait... are we still in the same place?!' he laughed in surprise.

'Yep!' said Molly, glancing at him briefly.

Tim was relieved to spot a quick smile flash across her face.

Huh... maybe he'd crack this one yet!

Staring around, Tim blinked as his eyes started to adjust to the low light. They were in a long, low, stone-lined passageway - complete with iron torch sconces on the walls. Every twenty feet or so, carved stone arches reached overhead. Following the great sweeping curves of the nearest one, he spotted the carving of an angel and a demon locked in battle overhead.

'Wow!' he gasped.

Realising that Molly was already well ahead, Tim pottered after her, but he made slow progress as his eyes darted around, trying to take everything in.

Here and there, alcoves appeared in the deep stone walls. Each one held some kind of treasure - pottery, carvings, pieces of art and old books that looked like they hadn't been touched in centuries. Far from being placed with any care, they seemed to have been shoved into the gaps just to get them out of the way – and then abandoned. Cobwebs and dust were very much the order of the day.

'Wow!' he said again, finally catching up with Molly, who'd paused to wait for him. 'It's like a museum out here!'

'Yeah... if a museum was a cobweb-infested dumping ground!' she laughed.

'But these pieces... some of them look pretty special!' said Tim, peering closely at an ancient stone carving of a girl in pigtails milking a cow.

'I keep telling Joyce that,' said Molly, lowering her

voice. 'She could do something really special with this place. But…'

Molly petered off, and Tim raised his eyebrows.

'But…?' he prompted.

'I'm just the receptionist, cleaner and all-round dog's-body,' whispered Molly. 'What would I know?!'

'Gotcha!' said Tim, rolling his eyes.

'Anyway, follow me,' said Molly.

At the end of the passageway, she led him through an arched doorway into a circular tower. An ancient spiral staircase curled upwards around the edge, its carved handrail damaged and chipped away in places. The stone treads of the stairs were worn too - polished smooth by the footfall of centuries.

'You need to watch your step on these, okay?' she said. 'They can be a bit tricky.'

'Okay, cheers,' he said with a nod

Tim followed Molly as she started to climb, his eyes still darting around in wonder. He'd just spotted a line of gargoyles about ten steps up!

They were halfway up the tower when disaster struck. Tim should have known it was coming, considering how distracted he was. He was doing anything but "watching his step" – what with the combination of ancient carvings every few feet and the shapely behind climbing the stairs just in front of him.

One minute, Tim was eyeballing an angel carved into the grey stone next to him, and the next, his foot slipped.

Before he knew what was happening, Tim felt his stomach swoop as his balance deserted him. Flailing and grabbing for the bannister to steady himself - Tim heard a strange squeak. It took a heartbeat to realise that the sound was coming from his own mouth. The section of bannister he'd just reached for was missing – crumbled away to nothing.

Tim grabbed at thin air and then felt himself lurch backwards, his heavy backpack teaming up with gravity.

This was going to hurt.

CHAPTER 5

MOLLY

Molly wasn't sure what had made her turn around. Perhaps it was the surprised squeak - or maybe the faint rustle of clothes sliding through thin air. Either way – she had a handful of Tim's jacket and jumper scrunched up in her balled fist. She'd somehow managed to grab him a split second before he'd plunged backwards.

Molly could feel his heart hammering directly beneath her fingertips – and their eyes were locked. Tim was still leaning backwards at a precarious angle - his heavy pack dangling from his shoulders. It was still threatening to drag him out of her grip if she wasn't careful.

'You okay?' she said, not daring to budge an inch in case their delicate balance shifted and they both lost their footing.

Tim blinked up at her. His face had completely drained of colour.

'Erm... yeah?' he said. 'I think so. How... how did you do that?'

Molly shook her head slightly and tightened her grip on him, her arm straining against the weight. If she was being perfectly honest, she'd been so deliciously aware of him following her up the stairs that she'd sensed the shift of air and sudden space behind her the moment he'd lost his footing. Pure instinct had made her wheel around and reach to grab him even before her brain had processed the fact that he was falling.

Thank goodness she had. She doubted his rucksack would have done much to cushion the fall.

'Here!' she said, planting her feet more firmly. 'Grab my other hand.'

Tim did as he was told and with one solid yank towards her, Molly dragged him back upright.

'Thank you!' he gasped, his eyes wide as he leaned heavily against the rough stone wall, breathing hard. 'Blimey, my heart!' he gasped, his voice shaky as his eyes slid back down the tower, clearly assessing just how far he would have fallen.

Molly couldn't help but shiver as she followed his gaze.

'You okay?' she said again, doing her best to keep her voice as calm as possible despite the fact that she could still feel his heart hammering. He looked a bit like he might pass out - not that she could blame him. She'd been nagging Joyce to get this staircase fixed for months now. Years, even. It was a disaster waiting to happen.

Tim nodded, and Molly saw his Adam's apple bob up and down a couple of times.

'Thanks!' he said again. 'I just – completely lost my footing!'

'Easily done,' said Molly with a nod. 'I've nearly gone the same way plenty of times – especially dragging the blasted vacuum cleaner up here!'

'Nice reflexes, by the way!' said Tim, his cheeky smile peeping through again – much to Molly's relief. It might not be back to full wattage just yet, but it was getting there.

He really was a nice-looking guy! His hat had fallen off in the drama, and a mop of dark, curly hair stood practically on end. He looked like he might be around the same age as her... maybe a little bit older... and he definitely had a few years on the other students.

Molly couldn't help herself as she swept her eyes over him. Standing this close was doing something funny to her. He smelled of wood smoke and something sweet. Maybe ginger? He must be pretty tall too... considering he was two steps below her but was still able to look her right in the eye!

He had nice eyes. *Really* nice eyes. Soft, melting brown... and that smile... now that he was starting to get the colour back in his cheeks – that smile was enough to leave *her* gasping for air instead of him!

It had been a *long* since anyone as hot as this had set foot inside the conference centre. Most of them were either grubby students like the others in Tim's party - kids who came to the island seeking adventure away from their parents - or delegates who turned up for the wine festival. Most of them tended to be quite a bit older… and preferred to stay with Olive at the Tallyaff. Not that she could blame them!

'Erm… I think I'm okay now,' said Tim.

'Huh?' said Molly, blinking rapidly and doing her best not to look like she'd been ogling him in his time of need.

'I think you can let go,' he chuckled, glancing down at her hand which still had a very firm grip on the front of his clothing. 'I promise not to throw myself off the staircase again!'

'Oh!' she said, removing her hand as though she'd just been scalded. 'Sorry!'

'Oooh no!' he laughed. 'You *seriously* don't need to apologise for saving me from crashing to my death!'

'Hardly your death!' she huffed, rolling her eyes in an attempt to gloss over the fact that she'd just gone strangely hot at the sight of his dimples. For one brief, crazy moment, she wanted to grab hold of him again, drag him towards her and kiss him. 'I mean… over-reaction, much!'

Tim snorted good-naturedly. 'Fine… maybe not my

death... but I'd definitely need a visit to your first aid box!'

'Yeah... you might have a point, there!' said Molly, turning away from him before she did something to disgrace herself. 'Ready to see your room?'

Molly paused, waiting for a reply. When none came, she turned back to him again to check he was okay, only to find him staring at her with wide eyes.

'What?' she said, raising an eyebrow.

'Nothing!' he said, hoisting his pack again. 'Just... interested to see what it's like compared to the cabins!'

'Well... you were a bit of a last-minute addition... so...' she trailed off.

'Right!' he laughed. 'I'm sure it'll be grand. I mean... I'm just glad you didn't take me down to the dungeons! I half wondered if you were going to chain me up and have your wicked way with me!'

Molly bit her lip, mainly to stop a snort of amusement from escaping. Tim was suddenly looking horrified – and luckily he was too busy turning bright red to notice she was struggling to keep herself from laughing.

'You wish!' she managed to grunt at last. 'Come on.'

Molly took a couple of steps at an ill-advised trot - given what had just happened. She just wanted to put a bit of space between them - because she was suddenly *very* aware that he was at eye level with her behind.

'You're just up here,' she threw over her shoulder,

climbing the last couple of steps before stopping in front of a large, studded wooden door.

'Wow!' said Tim, catching up with her.

'You ain't seen nothing yet!' she said, before using her thumb to loosen the old-fashioned catch. Pushing the door wide open, Molly kept her eyes on Tim's face, watching for his reaction.

Yup - there it was!

CHAPTER 6

TIM

Spectacular.
That was the word that came to mind as Tim stared around the huge, circular tower bedroom. It was unlike anything he'd seen so far at the Crumcarey Conference Centre. The portacabins had been... gross. That was really the only word for them. It wasn't just what they looked like either... there had been a distinct smell of damp and decaying Formica to them.

As for the castle, the little reception with its bare plasterboard had been completely unfinished – a perennial building site. The older parts Molly had just led him through had been magnificent in a dusty, cobwebby kind of way... but only if abandoned buildings were your thing.

This room though? This was unexpectedly gorgeous.

Tim's eyes darted around the space, trying to take it

all in. The centrepiece was a vast, canopied bed - its drapes boasting rich stripes of forest green, burnt orange and metallic gold that glinted under the soft lights. The bedding itself was a crisp, inviting white – and the comforter that was folded across the foot of the bed echoed the colours of the drapes.

Aware that Molly was watching him closely, Tim quickly tore his eyes away from the four-poster. That was definitely *not* safe territory right now. Instead, he glanced up at the ceiling – admiring a stunning array of vaulted oak timbers.

'This is…'

'Unexpected?' chuckled Molly from the doorway.

'Amazing!' said Tim. 'This is amazing!' He was still half-expecting to come to his senses and find himself standing inside a grotty portacabin instead.

'There's an ensuite through there,' said Molly, pointing towards another heavy, wooden door.

Tim wandered over and pulled it open, only to come face-to-face with a vast roll-top bath and a pyramid of fluffy white towels – all carefully rolled and piled onto an antique wooden trolly. Lush green house plants trailed from pots set on the deep stone windowsills, and the room smelled of oranges and cloves.

'Is this… is this really for me?' said Tim, closing the bathroom door again and turning to stare at Molly.

'All yours, Mr To Be Confirmed!' she said with a smile. 'But… can you do me a favour?'

'Anything!' said Tim sincerely.

'If you wouldn't mind avoiding telling the others?' she said. 'I think we'd have a mutiny on our hands if they found out, don't you?'

'Yeah, you're right!' laughed Tim. 'No worries, your secret is definitely safe with me. I won't tell the others.'

'Especially Professor McGrumpyPants?' added Molly, clearly keen to make sure he was taking her seriously.

'Yeah... especially him,' sniggered Tim. 'The guy already doesn't like me. I don't think this would do anything to help my cause!'

'You're probably right!' laughed Molly. 'I mean... no one's going to see you through the windows all the way up here, so you're safe there.'

Tim turned and made his way over to the mullioned panes, set into the deep stone walls. There was a custom-made set of curved wooden shutters that could be pulled across to block out the light - not that he was likely to use them... the view from up here was spectacular! Sure, it was still bucketing it down out there, but from up here, he could see how the blankets of cloud had turned the light a soft lavender-gold.

'I've even got a view of the standing stones!' he said, spotting them not too far off. 'Wow!'

'It's a good view, that's for sure,' said Molly. 'It's a shame more people don't get to stay up here!'

'Why not?' said Tim. 'I mean... it's gorgeous!'

'I agree!' said Molly. 'But it's the only room that's

been renovated. This was Joyce's last-gasp attempt at making the place up-scale.'

'But?' said Tim, completely confused... because as far as he could see, the woman was definitely on the right track!

'But,' said Molly, 'she blew the rest of her budget on a bunch of totally random, unnecessary stuff. So instead of gaining an entire renovated tower full of gorgeous rooms and a staircase that didn't try to bump off our guests – she ended up with one finished room and an empty bank account with no way to recoup the cash!'

'Shame!' said Tim. 'I mean... can you imagine if the rest of the place was done up like this? It'd be world-famous!'

'Yeah... I know,' sighed Molly.

Tim glanced at her and – by the strained look on her face - realised he'd just managed to stumble into a rather sore subject.

'Anyway,' said Molly, visibly straightening up and pulling herself together, 'I hope you've got everything you need up here – but just for the record, Joyce didn't tell me we had guests arriving until this morning. I had less than an hour to prepare the rooms before I had to come and pick you guys up... so if you're missing anything, just yell!'

'There's got to be some kind of drawback?' said Tim, staring around the room again. 'Is the bath just for show or something? Not plumbed in?'

'No!' Molly laughed in surprise. 'It's superb! The hot water comes from a boiler in the broom cupboard next door. It was meant to serve the entire tower - so there's always tons of hot water when it's on. No need to wait for creaky old pipes.'

'And the others just have those awful showers in the caravans!' said Tim, crinkling his nose.

'I mean… you *can* share your bathroom if you really want to…' said Molly.

'You've got to be kidding me?' said Tim.

Molly grinned at him. 'Yep.'

'Phew!' he laughed.

'I switched the boiler on for you earlier when I brought up fresh towels,' said Molly, 'so there should be hot water whenever you need it. And… as for the downside - you've already discovered it.'

'The bed!' said Tim, shaking his head. 'Tiny!'

'Don't even joke,' said Molly with a smirk. 'I think it could probably fit five people at a push.'

'Over my dead body!' said Tim. 'That bunch of unwashed kids? I don't think so!'

'Fair enough,' said Molly, wrinkling her nose. 'It's really nice though - soft and firm and… I don't know. It's super comfy… I'm not quite sure how to describe it.'

'No worries!' said Tim, starting to toe his boots off. As far as he was concerned, there was only one way to test out the comfort of a bed. 'One question?' he said, kicking his discarded shoes behind him.

'What's that?' said Molly, raising her eyebrows.

'The bedstead,' he said.

'What about it?' she asked.

'Is it old and full of woodworm?' he said, keeping his face straight with some difficulty.

'No!' said Molly, looking affronted. 'Joyce had a carpenter carve a new one based on the remains of one of the originals. It's new - but a pretty good imitation and…'

'So it can handle a bit of jumping around?' said Tim, trying and failing to keep his lips from twitching in amusement.

'Erm… what *exactly* are you suggesting?!' said Molly, turning a beautiful shade of pink.

'This!' said Tim with a grin and, before she could say anything else, he took a running jump towards the massive bed, diving onto the mattress.

'WOOHOO!' he giggled, jumping about and testing out the springs like a five-year-old on a sugar high. 'Care to join me?' he chuckled breathlessly, not pausing in his trampolining.

Molly's pink face went from disbelief to disapproval, and then all the way around to pure temptation in a matter of seconds. Luckily – temptation won. Tim watched as she slipped out of her own shoes before clambering onto the mattress beside him.

'Soft and firm!' giggled Tim.

'Soft and firm!' Molly nodded, bouncing around on her knees for a couple of seconds before losing her balance and toppling backwards into the pillows. 'Oops!'

Tim turned to her, and his heart did a weird kind of backflip. For one brief moment, the stressed-out frown lines that had been present from the moment Molly had picked them up in the knackered minibus had disappeared. She'd closed her eyes, and her dark hair was spread out across the crisp, white pillowcase in a halo.

Molly let out a contented sigh, and Tim felt his heart turn to something resembling hot caramel sauce. Not wanting to be caught in the act of ogling her, he quickly flopped down onto the other pillow and let out his own happy sigh.

'This is a good room!' he murmured on a yawn.

'You wait till you see the view set against the sunrise,' said Molly. 'The stone circle looks even better when there isn't a curtain of rain in the way!'

'Nice,' said Tim, making a snap decision not to air his thoughts about the possibility that it might be fake. He didn't want to be *that* know-it-all guest! 'Well… thanks for the preferential treatment!'

Molly's eyes flew open, and she quickly scrambled back off the bed. Tim kicked himself as he watched her slip her shoes on, her professional mask sliding back into place.

Damnit! Why couldn't he keep his mouth shut?!

Now she was going to go… and it wasn't like he

could invite her back to bed, was it? That would be more than a bit inappropriate!

'Right,' she said, 'breakfast is served from seven in the morning in the Dining Hall. Don't get too excited, though,' she added quickly. 'It'll be… basic.'

'No room service?' he said lightly, making one more play for that lovely smile of hers. It didn't work - all he got was an eye-roll.

'Up that staircase? You've got to be kidding me!' she huffed. 'I'll… erm… leave you to settle in, then.'

Tim watched regretfully as Molly backed out of the room, closing the door gently behind her.

Ah well – it was time to look on the bright side. He had a beautiful room - and there was bound to be plenty of time to find out more about the mysterious Molly. At least there was *something* here on Crumcarey that had captured his interest!

CHAPTER 7

MOLLY

Resisting the urge to slump back against the closed door, Molly began to pick her way carefully back down the spiral staircase. She felt… funny. Stirred up and giddy… and more than a little bit stupid.

What on earth had she been playing at - diving onto the bed with a complete stranger and jumping around like a toddler?! He was a guest, for goodness sake! She could lose her job!

It was hard enough to keep any semblance of professionalism in this place as it was – what with the conference centre quite literally crumbling around her ears. Did she really need to add to that by misbehaving with the guests?

Okay - *guest*.

Molly had never done anything like that before - and she wouldn't again, either. She needed to keep her boundaries up when it came to Mr Tim *To-Be-Confirmed* Stewart!

As she sidled past the gap in the bannisters, Molly wondered briefly whether she should admit to Joyce what had just happened. It took all of three seconds before she thought better of it. For one thing... it hadn't been "jumping *into* bed" with a guest, had it? More like jumping *on* the bed with a guest.

Joyce didn't need to know. Molly might not know much about Tim - but she didn't think he was the kind of bloke to snitch on her. In fact... he'd looked like he was enjoying himself!

Molly permitted herself a tiny smile as she thought about the pure joy on his cheeky, handsome face as he'd tested out the mattress next to her. She'd wanted to do that ever since the room had been renovated and the vast bed had been carried up there. *That* had taken some doing - Joyce had somehow roped in Olive's husband and Connor the ferry captain for the job.

No - it was no good! It didn't matter how she tried to swing it... bouncing up and down on a bed with a guest was a bad idea – no matter how cute his dimples were!

'When did you become so boring, Molly Mackenzie?' she muttered, trotting the rest of the way down the staircase.

It was true. She'd definitely lost her spark recently. That indescribable *something* that made you wiggle with excitement. Her wiggle had... disappeared, and she had a feeling it had something to do with the weight of keeping this place going. The wine festival was the only thing that kept the conference centre afloat - and it always landed squarely on her shoulders. That definitely didn't help her feel light and fluffy - or wiggly!

Anyway – even if she'd forgotten how to have fun – that was no excuse. Just because a hot guy had taken up residence in the tower room, it didn't mean she could forget about all her boundaries! Sure, decent blokes on the island had been in pretty short supply of late, but did she really have to act like a sex-starved idiot?

Nope. She didn't!

Still, she'd prefer to stay lounging around with Mr Dimples in the tower room than go back down to the depressing reception.

'Pull yourself together, Molly!' she said, yanking a smile back onto her face. 'You're meant to be running a conference centre.'

Not mooning around after a guest. No matter how cute he is!

Taking a deep breath and praying that none of the students would be waiting for her on the other side of the door, Molly pushed her way through.

'There you are!'

Balls!

Molly had been so caught up with thoughts of Tim that she'd completely forgotten to worry about bumping into Joyce.

Her boss usually stayed well out of the way when they had visitors - mainly because being anywhere near them meant that she might end up doing some work by mistake. Here she was though, looking as wide-eyed and scatty as usual. In fact, it looked very much like Joyce had already changed into a pair of tartan PJ bottoms – which looked quite bizarre teamed up with her blazer jacket.

'Hi!' said Molly, forcing a polite smile onto her face.

It wasn't that Molly disliked the woman. After all, Joyce had given her a job – something that was decidedly rare on Crumcarey. On top of that, she was nice enough... most of the time.

The problem was - Molly adored this old place - the castle and the grounds, at least. If it was hers, she'd be doing things very differently... but of course, it wasn't... and she couldn't.

The fact that Molly cared about the place meant it was incredibly difficult to watch as guests were grossed out by the horrific portacabins and disintegrating toilet block. The beautiful old castle just got ignored... and before long, it would be too far gone for anyone to be able to save.

Molly shook her head, pushing these pointless thoughts to the back of her mind. There was nothing she could do about any of it right now, so there was no point dwelling on it, was there?!

'Where have you been?!' said Joyce, looking mildly harassed.

'Erm… showing our guests to their rooms?' said Molly, doing her best not to look guilty.

After all - that's what she was meant to be doing. Joyce didn't know that she'd been enjoying her job a little bit more than usual while bounding around on the tower bed, did she?

'I had to take one of the students up to the tower room,' she added. 'As you know… we're full!'

'Right, right…' said Joyce, gazing around the ugly reception as though she was surprised to find herself there. 'Thing is, Molly, I'm not happy.'

Molly's stomach lurched. Maybe Joyce *did* know what she'd been up to after all!

'Oh - what's up?' she said, doing her best to look innocent.

'Why didn't you put the professor in the tower room?!' demanded Joyce. Suddenly, she looked a lot less fluffy. Joyce's gaze locked on Molly – and she squirmed. Huh… that definitely wasn't the ditzy Joyce she was used to dealing with!

'Well… I was just following your orders,' said Molly, thinking fast. 'I mean… if our guests know they can ask for the tower room every time they come here, it's the only room that would get used. And… like you said, it's expensive to run… new towels, new boiler… heating… all that!'

Joyce tilted her head and narrowed her eyes. 'But… this lot are already here!'

Molly swallowed. She couldn't exactly tell Joyce she

didn't put the old git in there because he was an unpleasant know-it-all and she'd wanted to take him down a peg or two, could she?

'Yeah... but there was one name on the list that was still to be confirmed,' she said. 'I thought... if they hadn't filled the spot, we could leave the tower room empty and save you some cash!'

Joyce blinked at her slowly and then nodded.

'Okay. Good girl,' she said. 'Good thinking. Sadly - it wasn't to be - and now we've got a smelly student up there!'

'Right,' said Molly, biting her lip to stop herself from laughing. Tim didn't smell bad... kind of outdoorsy... fresh air and woodsmoke mixed with that hint of ginger...

'Well anyway,' continued Joyce, 'I just bumped into the professor and we had a little chat. We've got a bit of a problem.'

Uh oh! That couldn't be good.

'Oh?' said Molly. They'd definitely have a problem if Joyce had spilled the beans about the tower room. She didn't doubt that the old buffer would throw Tim out of there without a second thought. 'You didn't tell him about the tower, did you?'

'Erm...' said Joyce, 'I don't think so. I can't really remember... it doesn't really matter, does it?'

Molly shook her head and smiled even though it was the last thing she felt like doing. If Joyce had ratted her out, it wasn't her boss who'd have to deal with the fallout.

'So… what's the problem?' said Molly

'Well,' she said, rubbing her face and looking anxious all of a sudden, 'it's really important you don't breathe a single word to *any* of them about those standing stones being fake.'

Molly raised her eyebrows in surprise. 'They're here to study the stones?'

'They are,' said Joyce. Once again, Molly noticed she was looking anything but fluffy.

'I thought they might be here because of this place,' said Molly. 'The castle… the grounds…'

'Don't be ridiculous!' laughed Joyce. 'This place? No - they're here for the stones. According to the professor, they could be of some real scientific interest, and…'

'But… Mr McCluskey put those up in the middle of the night as an April Fool's joke!' spluttered Molly, completely unable to contain a giggle. 'I remember it - just about. I was still at school. Mum and dad took me over to see them the next day. I think I've still got the photos somewhere. You can still see some of the tyre tracks from his tractor!'

'Shh!' said Joyce, her eyes flying wide as she turned to glance nervously at the door. 'Keep your voice down, girl!'

'But-?' laughed Molly. 'But - surely you're going to tell them?'

'Over my dead body!' muttered Joyce. 'If the man's idiot enough to think they're real, I'm not going to put him straight… and neither are you. He said he's planning to bring more students back here every year for the foreseeable future. This is just the first part of the funding he's secured… and it's all very exciting.'

'But…?' said Molly.

Surely this man was supposed to be an expert? Surely he'd know within seconds of taking a proper look at the stones that the whole thing was a hoax… a fake… a giant, island-wide joke?

'But *nothing*, Molly,' hissed Joyce. 'We need this. We need guests, and I'll take them any way I can get them. He's the expert. If he's made a mistake, I'll let him figure it out in his own time… and take his cash while he's at it!'

'But…!' said Molly again. This was getting ridiculous.

'No. No buts,' said Joyce, her voice stern. 'You want to keep your job? Keep your mouth shut. Understand?'

Molly opened her mouth to argue again, but then shut it again and just nodded.

'Good girl!' said Joyce, giving her arm a quick pat. 'Now, the group are going to meet up tomorrow morning in the Dining Hall to discuss where to start with the dig.'

'Okay,' said Molly, feeling more than a little bit uncomfortable.

'I want the professor to know how important his

business is to me,' she said. 'So I want you on hand to greet them... and then take them over to the stones in person. Call Olive and get her to provide a decent breakfast for the first day. Pastries. Make some decent tea and coffee. You can switch over to the cheap stuff the day after. Grab what you need from the Tallyaff first thing.'

'Really?' said Molly.

Normally, Joyce was all too happy to let their guests fend for themselves. A couple of packets of slightly soft cereal and not quite enough milk to go around was usually the extent of the breakfasts she served.

'Really!' said Joyce. 'I want you at his beck and call this week, got it? Whatever that group needs, you sort it out... as long as it doesn't cost anything. Just... be there, okay?'

Molly nodded. Blimey - she'd better start practising keeping a straight face. Something told her it was going to be seriously hard work not to get the giggles while they all investigated Mr McCluskey's April Fool handiwork!

CHAPTER 8

TIM

*S*oft light seeped into the room, and Tim turned over in bed, snuggling deeper under the cosy cotton covers as he stared up at the canopy overhead.

Wait... canopy?

This wasn't his room in his shared student flat!

Sitting up abruptly, Tim let his eyes roam around the unfamiliar room... and a huge smile spread across his face.

Of course!

He was in the most beautiful bedroom he'd ever set eyes on, in the most comfortable bed he'd ever had the pleasure of sleeping in. This canopied four-poster was a thing of dreams... and he was already dreading leaving it behind when it came time to leave.

Tim had slept like a log - not that there was anything unusual about that – but he'd never had the chance to do it in such style and comfort before! Plus... there had been the dreams. Snatches of dark hair tumbling across the pillows... and Molly's laughing face as she'd bounced around on the mattress next to him.

Right... enough of that! Otherwise, he'd be needing a cold shower before heading downstairs to join the rest of them for breakfast.

Urgh... the rest of them!

Just the thought of his professor and classmates brought Tim back down to earth with a bump. No matter how glorious his room had turned out to be - and no matter what an unexpected surprise Molly was - he wasn't here for a five-star holiday with a beautiful woman, was he? He was here to investigate a bunch of decidedly questionable standing stones.

'Wild goose chase, I reckon!' he chuckled, throwing the covers off with a pang of regret.

Remembering what Molly had said about the view in the early morning, Tim hauled himself off the mattress and padded over towards the window. Sliding the heavy drapes out of the way, he leaned across the deep sill and gently pulled the curved wooden shutters open.

'Wow!' he gasped.

The view that met his eyes was enough to bring a grown man to tears. The sun was just peeping over the horizon and the sea in the distance had turned into a line of rose-gold fire. Billowing storm clouds glowed as they framed the edges of the scene. Right in the middle – set against this glorious backdrop - were the standing stones. They cast long, low shadows over the rough island grassland.

Tim sucked in a deep breath as the hairs on the back of his neck and arms rose with a tingle of delight

What a view!

Well… there they were. The stones. The reason he was here on Crumcarey in the first place. He had to admit – even if his suspicions turned out to be true and they weren't some kind of archaeological discovery of the century – they still looked pretty impressive.

Tim ruffled his hair, fidgeting slightly. Surely Professor Estwick had done more background research than he was giving him credit for?

Either way – Tim was determined to keep his suspicions about the stones to himself. He'd already tried to flag up the anomalies between the photographs in the book and the ones the professor's mum had taken - and it had gone down like a lead balloon.

What would he know? This was only his second term of the course, and Professor Estwick had already told him that he wasn't a "true archaeologist" at heart.

Tim shrugged. He didn't really care what the professor thought of him. He was more than prepared to muck in with the others and do what needed to be done. He didn't mind being out in the elements… wind, rain and snow held no fear for him. Not with his trusty waterproofs on, anyway!

He reached up and stretched, his eyes still glued to the spectacular view in front of him. He didn't dare look away. It was changing by the second, the shadows shifting as the clouds drifted on the wind, turning the beams of gold into a glittering lightshow across the landscape. He might not have volunteered to be here, but right now he wouldn't want to be anywhere else on earth.

Now that he'd met Molly, Tim was all-in. She was so… unexpected. For some reason, he couldn't quite get a read on her. She was serious one minute and playful the next. He definitely hadn't wanted her to go the previous evening – in fact, he'd come embarrassingly close to begging her to stay for a drink. He probably would have if he'd had anything to offer her other than tap water!

Tim couldn't wait to see her again!

Once again, the hairs on the back of his arms stood to attention and Tim laughed out loud. It was like his body was sensing some kind of major shift…

'Or maybe you're just cold, idiot!' he chuckled, giving himself a shake.

Tim usually prided himself on being practical and pragmatic. Clearly, something about sleeping in the tower of a castle and getting to watch the sunrise had stirred up romantic notions in his usually down-to-earth brain! Here he was, standing around in just a tee shirt and a pair of boxer shorts, wondering why he was shivering.

It was definitely time to get dressed and face the music!

It took Tim all of three minutes to wash, dress and leave his gorgeous bedroom reluctantly behind him. He'd lounged around in the magnificent bath for an age the previous evening... but he didn't dare draw himself another one right now, otherwise he might not emerge again until well past lunchtime!

Reaching the top of the stairs, Tim swallowed down his excitement about possibly getting to see Molly again and took the steps slowly and carefully. As much as he wanted to bound down them - the last thing he wanted to do was end up in a heap at the bottom with a broken bone or two. That wouldn't be a good look!

As soon as he reached the bottom in one piece, Tim retraced his steps from the day before. He headed along the stone corridor with its cobwebby wonders and then pushed his way back into the horrible interior of the plasterboard reception with its sad-looking trestle table and plastic chairs. It was a bit like stepping out of a fairy tale into a nightmare, and Tim wrinkled his nose as the sense of being surrounded by magic promptly deserted him.

The reception was empty, and he hurried over towards the door Molly had pointed out the precious day that led to the Dining Hall.

'Here goes nothing!' he sighed, giving the handle an experimental tug. It opened with a tired groan, leaving a little snowstorm of raw plaster in its wake.

Blimey, this place was in serious need of some TLC! Tim was sure his mum had said a really swanky wine festival took place here every year... but right now, he was having a hard time picturing it.

Well, he wasn't going to spend any time trying to work out that particular puzzle right now. He needed some breakfast before spending all day outside. No doubt the professor would have some lousy job for him to do... like clearing sheep-poo off the site or something.

Ducking under the low doorframe, Tim made his way along a corridor that was made up of more plasterboard, held in place by a bunch of rough, raw wooden batons. The huge flagstones underfoot were the only hint that he was still inside the same castle.

At the far end of the corridor was another door - this one made up of rough planks, haphazardly held together with what looked like a bunch of offcuts that should really have been put in the bin.

Tim gave it a gentle push – not trusting it to hold up against anything more forceful – and sidled through the gap. Then he came to a crashing halt.

When Molly had said breakfast would be served in the "Dining Hall", he'd thought it was just a turn of phrase. He'd been wrong – very wrong – because here he was, standing at one end of a huge feasting hall.

Just like the spiral staircase up to his room, the flagstones in here had been worn smooth. The same rose-gold morning light that had greeted him up in the tower flooded in through mullioned windows that were set along the entire side of the hall. At the far end of the room was the largest fireplace Tim had ever set eyes on and it was roaring with warmth - the flickering flames illuminating the faces of his classmates.

'Morning!' he called, heading towards them.

Faces turned to greet him… and every single one of them looked dreadful. Pale, scruffy and exhausted – the others looked dead on their feet. The professor had bags under his eyes the size of suitcases. He looked knackered… and more than usually grumpy.

Tim promptly did his best not to look too smug and well-rested. It was obvious that this lot hadn't managed to get a wink of sleep between them.

Something told him that the horrific communal shower room Molly had shown them the day before wouldn't be seeing much action this week. For one brief moment, Tim felt incredibly guilty about the ginormous claw-footed bathtub he was very much looking forward to soaking in again at the end of the day! Of course, a decent person would own up to the fact that he had the most beautiful room in the whole place… and might even offer to share the facilities with the others.

Clearly, he *wasn't* a decent person… and he was fine with that!

'You guys get some breakfast?' he asked as he came to stand between Rosie with her blue topknot - which was looking a bit sad and deflated this morning - and

Rhodri, who'd pulled his beanie down so low it looked like he was considering taking a nap at any moment.

'Over there,' yawned Rosie, pointing towards a trestle table Tim hadn't noticed because he'd been too busy gawking at the stunning space. 'There are pastries and the girl has gone for coffee.'

'Oh right - cheers!' he said with a grin.

'Hurry up, man,' grumbled the professor. 'I want to make a start.'

Tim shrugged and strolled at a leisurely pace over towards the table. They were still missing a couple of the other students - and he knew he was at least ten minutes early for their meeting. There was no need to rush - it was just the professor being a git – as usual.

Staring at the food laid out on the table, Tim was surprised to find so much on offer. There was a small mountain of pastries, a bowl of fresh fruit, sliced bread piled next to a toaster, and enough jam, marmalade and butter to sink a battleship. Basic… but yum!

Tim reached out, grabbed a paper plate, and helped himself to a chocolate pastry from the pile, his mouth watering in anticipation.

'Morning,' came a quiet voice from behind him.

Tim felt the familiar tingle on the back of his neck again. Turning slowly, he came face to face with Molly, who was brandishing a huge thermal jug.

'Can I tempt you?' she said, her lovely lilting voice making him go instantly weak at the knees. He'd thought she was cute last night, but as the rosy glow of the rising sun flooded in through the windows, it touched her hair, igniting a thousand golden lights in the dark waves.

'Huh?' he said, his brain instantly empty of anything but her.

'Coffee?' she laughed, waggling the jug.

'Right… right…' he gasped. 'Please!'

CHAPTER 9

MOLLY

Her plan had been to get in and out of the hall with the pot of coffee before the professor made a start on his meeting. After all, Molly didn't really want to be in there when he started waffling on about the stones.

For one thing... she might start laughing - and that would be a disaster considering the warning Joyce had given her. For another... she had a feeling she wouldn't be able to keep her eyes off a certain Mr To-Be-Confirmed.

But... plans be damned.

Molly had been standing behind Tim for several long minutes, watching as he eyeballed the breakfast table with a look of pure appreciation. She'd started to feel a bit awkward about the fact that she was basically just standing there, ogling him and decided she'd better break the silence before one of the other students - or even worse, the professor - came over to join them.

'Morning!' she said.

Tim turned and Molly almost dropped the jug of fresh coffee as those dimples made their morning appearance.

'Huh?' he said, blinking at her.

Well – he certainly looked a lot better rested than the rest of them!

'Coffee?' she said, waggling the pot at him.

'Right... right... please!' he said, smiling at her.

Molly nodded and grabbed one of the larger mugs from the table, pouring him a steaming vat of the stuff. *Not* that she was playing favourites or anything!

'Thanks,' he said, flashing a smile at her.

Molly found herself smiling right back - a wide, warm beam she had precisely zero control over. The fact that there was a gaggle of unkempt, knackered students huddled over by the fire - along with a decidedly disgruntled-looking professor – simply didn't matter. Right now, the guy standing in front of her tucking into one of the pastries as though his life depended on it had her undivided attention.

'Oh my goodness,' sighed Tim after taking a sip of coffee. 'Heaven!'

Molly chuckled. That was exactly how she reacted to her first coffee of the day too... but never out loud, and definitely not when she was in company. Tim seemed to be missing the usual filters when it came to being enthusiastic, childlike and playful. He just let it all show - no matter who was around. She had to admit, it was probably one of the most attractive things she'd ever witnessed.

'If you two are *quite* done with the canoodling over there, I'd like to get this session started!' came the professor's testy voice. Clearly, the man didn't do too well after a night spent in the less-than-lovely guest accommodation!

Molly opened her mouth to apologise, but promptly shut it again as she caught Tim's apologetic eye roll in her direction. She didn't trust herself not to start giggling.

'Sorry!' said Tim, turning towards the professor and toasting him with his steaming mug. 'I wasn't canoodling with anything other than this coffee, though... and you really need to get in on the action... it'll make you weak at the knees!'

Molly let out a snort before she could stop herself and quickly turned her back on the group as a couple of students started to laugh. She badly wanted to join in with them, but somehow she didn't think it'd look too professional to gang up on the professor with Tim and the others.

'Mr Stewart, please join us,' snapped the professor. 'You are holding up the entire group.'

Molly ducked her head as though it was a physical blow aimed at her, rather than a petty barb tossed at Tim. She shot a glance in his direction - but other than the fact that his smile had gone a bit stiff - he didn't seem to be too bothered.

'Okay, fine,' he replied. 'But you're missing out!'

Rather than heading over to join the group though, Tim turned to Molly and shot her a wink. Then he hefted the coffee jug, topped his mug up, grabbed a second pastry - and only then did he amble over towards the others.

Molly bit her lip hard. Now she was *really* struggling to keep a straight face. She turned just in time to see the rest of the little group eyeballing his coffee. It was obvious they were all in desperate need of caffeine... but unlike Tim, they weren't brave enough to poke the bear... aka Professor Grumpy Pants!

'Fine,' she sighed quietly. 'I'll sort it out.'

Molly quickly gathered a bunch of mugs onto a tray, filled them with coffee and then added the little jug of milk and a sugar bowl. If they weren't allowed to come and help themselves, she'd take it to them... it'd be a complete waste otherwise!

As Molly sidled towards the group bearing the tray, she noticed that all of them – even Tim – already had identical glazed expressions on their faces. It wasn't exactly surprising though, given that the professor's voice had the kind of droning quality that was the vocal equivalent of watching paint dry. Actually, if she was being honest, that would probably be preferable to listening to him!

Coming to stand next to the girl with the blue topknot, Molly gave her a gentle nudge.

'Coffee?' she whispered.

The girl widened her eyes in surprise and then made a heart shape with her fingers at Molly before grabbing a mug. Then she gave the lad standing on the other side of her a subtle prod in the ribs and pointed towards the tray.

Within seconds, all the students were shuffling towards her, grabbing mugs and shooting her grateful smiles that made her think of a pack of lost puppy dogs.

'Young lady!' growled the professor as the final student let out an audible sigh after taking his first sip of coffee. 'You are disrupting our meeting.'

'Sorry,' muttered Molly. 'I just thought you might all like a drink before heading outside… and I thought this way would save you time.'

'Well… well…' blustered the professor, who was now eyeballing the last cup on her tray, clearly caught between the desire to continue telling her off and his own need to get some strong caffeine into his system. 'Well!' he said again.

'There's one left for you…' said Molly quietly, forcing herself not to catch Tim's eye - otherwise she'd be in serious danger of giving into the giggles that were still waiting in the wings. 'Only if you'd like it… or I can just pour it away?'

'No!' he gasped. 'Thank you. I'll take it - as you've already interrupted our meeting.'

Molly couldn't help it – she gave in and glanced at Tim, only to catch him in the middle of such an enthusiastic eye-roll, it wouldn't surprise her if he strained something in the process.

'Here,' she said, holding the tray out towards the professor. He took it with about as much grace as a crocodile with a toothache.

'Now then - you're welcome to listen in - but please do not interrupt,' he said, drawing himself up to his full height while carefully cradling his warm mug. 'We are gearing up to start a very important project - not that you'd understand. The standing stones here are wonderful. Uncharted history like this is-'

'I'll just leave you to it!' said Molly, pointing wildly towards the table where the breakfast buffet was laid out. She quickly turned and scuttled off. She knew she'd just been incredibly rude – cutting him off like that – but she'd had no other choice. Her shoulders were now shaking with suppressed laughter… and she wasn't going to be able to hold it in for much longer!

Molly darted for the table and grabbed blindly for the empty coffee jug. She'd head out to the kitchen and take a minute to compose herself. The professor was bound to waffle on for ages, so she'd have plenty of time to pull her outdoor gear on before she was needed again!

Just as she was making a dive for the doorway,

Molly heard the professor begin to explain the kind of artefacts they'd be hoping to find once the dig was underway.

'Artefacts, my ass!' chuckled Molly the minute she was out of the hall. The most they could hope to find were some bits of dead tractor, and maybe a buckle or two from McGregor's old collars - Mr Harris's scruffy little dog was always losing them. As for arrowheads, neolithic sculptures and votive hoards... he should be so lucky!

'What are you still doing here?'

Molly's laughter deserted her as she entered the kitchen and promptly came to a screeching halt. Joyce was leaning against the knackered Formica counter, nibbling on a piece of jam and toast.

'Just thought I'd bring this back out here - ready for more coffee when the group have their break,' she said quickly, thinking on her feet.

'Okay,' said Joyce with a shrug. 'How's it going out there? Is the professor happy? You're making sure he's got everything he needs, right?'

'I'm doing my best!' said Molly. 'Though I'm not sure I'd describe the man as happy. They're having a meeting about the stones at the moment... surely he's going to be gutted when he realises they're not even remotely worth studying?'

'Listen to me!' said Joyce, almost dropping her piece of toast. 'You aren't to drop even the slightest hint that those stones are anything other than ancient and mysterious. Got it?!'

'But...' said Molly. She was about to point out that it was all going to become pretty obvious very soon, but Joyce cut right across her.

'Don't you dare! If you do, you're fired,' said Joyce.

Molly gaped at her. That was the second time Joyce had threatened to get rid of her. Maybe she really meant it!

'It'll take them ages to figure anything out,' said Joyce. 'These people always move at a snail's pace because they're terrified of making a mess of a significant find, right?'

'Yes... but...'

'So, that means they'll be coughing up to stay here for donkey's yonks. This trip. Future trips. It could be the making of the place.'

'But it's based on a lie!' said Molly.

'Are you an expert in archaeology?' demanded Joyce, raising one thin, pencilled eyebrow.

'No but-'

'Neither am I – so what would we know?!' said Joyce. 'And in case you haven't noticed, I need the cash... I need this business. If you want to keep your job, you'll keep them happy – whatever it takes! Understand?'

Molly nodded slowly. She didn't like it any more than she had the previous day - but she didn't really have a choice in the matter, did she?!

'Good - now get back out there!' hissed Joyce, grabbing the jug from her.

It was as much as Molly could do to snag her wellington boots from under the counter before Joyce ushered her right out of the kitchen and straight back towards the hall.

CHAPTER 10

TIM

'Do you understand?' said the professor, staring at Tim with a smug smile dancing on his face.

Tim nodded. Of course he understood. The others had all been given their jobs - important roles around the base of the stones themselves. They'd be sketching, measuring and investigating the topography. He, however, was being sent off on his own on some kind of fool's errand to do with the local watercourses.

The thing the professor *didn't* seem to grasp was that he was more than happy with his assignment.

Thrilled, in fact.

It wasn't a huge surprise, of course. Tim had been expecting something like this. Professor Estwick didn't like him... and the fact that he'd got to the coffee before the rest of them really didn't seem to have helped matters.

All Tim had to do now was be careful not to look too enthusiastic about the whole thing - otherwise, the professor might change his mind. The man would hate to think he'd inadvertently managed to make him happy!

'Mr Stewart – I'm trusting you with this,' snapped the professor. 'Tell me what I want you to do – convince me you understand the assignment!'

Tim sighed. 'You want me to explore the local water courses - working away from the site - looking for items of interest,' he parroted.

'Exactly,' said the professor. 'I've got photocopies from the book here somewhere – you can use them as a guide.'

'I've got my own, don't worry,' said Tim, patting his pocket.

'Oh… well… good.'

The professor promptly turned his back on Tim, clearly glad to have washed his hands of him for the day.

Reining in the desire to stick his tongue out at the back of the man's head, Tim chanced a glance over towards Molly instead. He'd clocked her the moment she'd come back into the hall – and now she was sitting on an old wooden bench near the door, pulling her wellington boots on.

That was the only downside of being sent off on his own – Molly was going to be taking the rest of them to the standing stones - and he'd be going in the opposite direction. It was a shame because it meant he'd miss out on the chance to chat to her on the walk over there. Ah well – with any luck he'd bump into her later on instead.

'Right then,' said the professor, 'let's get out there.'

Tim breathed a sigh of relief. Fresh air. Daylight. Peace and quiet. It wouldn't be too bad, would it?!

'You ready for this?' muttered Tim, heading over to stand next to Molly. She grinned up at him, making his stomach squirm.

'*I* am,' she said, giving him a wink that made Tim seriously consider sitting down next to her before his knees gave out. 'Not sure about that lot, though,' she added nodding at the tired and bedraggled group making their way across the hall towards them.

∼

Tim watched as the little group set off around the back of the castle before climbing one at a time through a hole in the fence. Molly was taking them directly across the fields towards the standing stones.

'See ya!' sighed Tim with a little pang of regret.

If she wasn't busy babysitting that lot and making sure they didn't get lost down any rabbit holes, Tim would have invited her to come for a walk with him instead. Still… if he knew Professor Estwick as well as he thought he did, he had a feeling the old codger would be sending him off on his own for most of the trip. With any luck, he'd have plenty more chances to get to know Molly better!

Turning his back on the little group as they disappeared across the fields, Tim stared up at the sky. It was going to be a decidedly damp sort of a day by the looks of things. It might not be raining right now, but he knew enough about island weather to know that those clouds rolling towards him from the sea meant rain – somewhere on the island, at least. If it was anything like Brumeldsay, it could be raining in your front garden and dry and sunny in your back garden – the storms were that localised!

Tim didn't mind, though. What was a bit of rain? He was getting to spend a whole day outdoors - exploring a new place. Plus, he had decent waterproofs… unlike the others!

Setting out at a brisk pace, Tim headed down the uneven gravel driveway towards the road. His plan was to put a bit of distance between himself and his pompous, preening professor as quickly as possible.

Tim didn't bother pulling the old Crumcarey travel guide out of his pocket. The professor might be treating it like a bible – but Tim knew only too well that if he followed its directions, he'd be lost in minutes. After all, everything it described was on a completely different island - Brumeldsay! He wasn't even sure why he'd brought it with him - other than the fact it might provide a bit of a talking point if he *had* somehow managed to talk Molly into coming with him.

Tim had only been walking down the middle of the little road for about five minutes when he spotted something strange in the distance.

Surely... surely he had to be seeing things?!

A beam of sunlight cut through the clouds, and Tim let out a laugh. He wasn't making it up! There, with sunlight gleaming on its gorgeous custard, pink and cream paintwork, was an old ice cream van.

Maybe there had been something in that coffee Molly had served him for breakfast, and he was starting to hallucinate!

Picking up his pace, Tim didn't take his eyes off the van as he hurried towards it. It was pretty much the last thing he'd expected to find on a windswept, remote Scottish island on a stormy day in February – maybe even less likely than the ancient artefacts the professor was so sure he was going to discover!

The beautiful van was tucked into a passing place – and Tim couldn't resist having a closer look… even though he'd bet pretty much anything that there wasn't any actual ice cream on board.

Reaching the window, Tim tapped lightly on the glass. Up popped the very surprised-looking face of a woman. He watched as she slid back the window with a bemused expression on her face - and as she did so, a man appeared at her side.

'Hey!' she said, sounding slightly breathless. He'd

clearly made her jump. 'We didn't expect any customers today!'

'Sorry to bother you!' said Tim quickly.

'Not a bother at all,' she laughed. 'You're just unexpected!'

'Yeah!' said the guy standing next to her. 'We just decided to park up somewhere different... change of scenery, you know? Didn't think anyone would appear wanting ice cream!'

'That's if you wanted to buy anything, of course,' said the woman, digging the guy in the ribs with her elbow. 'No pressure.'

'You've seriously got ice cream?' said Tim, his eyes widening in delight.

'Well... duh!' laughed the woman. 'I mean, we *are* an ice cream van!'

'Then I'll be buying!' said Tim, patting his pocket just to check he had some change on him.

'I'm Stella, by the way,' said the woman, 'and this is Frank.'

'Tim!' he said with a grin.

'And what are you doing out here in the middle of nowhere?' said Frank with an easy smile.

'I'm with the group at the conference centre,' said Tim. 'I'm an archaeology student.'

'You guys here to study the old castle?' said Stella with interest.

'I wish,' sighed Tim. 'We're here for the stones.'

He watched in amusement as both sets of eyebrows

flew up. Frank glanced uneasily at Stella and then back at Tim.

'Don't worry,' he laughed, sensing the poor guy was doing his best not to put his foot in it. 'I know there's *something* off about them.'

'You could say that!' snorted Stella, before clapping her hand over her mouth, looking horrified.

'Don't worry on my account!' said Tim. 'Can you tell me anything about them?'

'I can tell you *everything* about them!' laughed Stella. 'Mr McCluskey put them up as an April Fool's joke… maybe… twenty years ago? Something like that!'

'Amazing!' chuckled Tim. The professor was going to be livid when he found out.

'They *are* very pretty,' said Frank fairly. 'And they make a great backdrop for tourist's photos.'

'Yeah,' said Stella cocking her head to one side. 'But most of us locals can still remember the night Mr McCluskey dragged them into the field with his rusty old tractor! He did a lovely job… but they're about as archaeologically significant as Ruby here.' She patted the old ice cream van affectionately.

'Looks like my professor's going to be in for a bit of a shock, then!' said Tim, unable to keep a huge grin from spreading across his face.

'Doesn't he already *know* something's off?' said Frank in surprise.

Tim shook his head. 'And *I'm* definitely not going to say anything!'

'Well... neither are we,' said Stella. 'Those stones are good for Crumcarey. They bring in tourists – and as Frank said, they do make a nice backdrop for weddings and celebrations. Though... it's pretty rare anyone stays at the conference centre these days.'

'I can see why,' said Tim before he could think better of it.

'Poor old Molly!' said Frank, shaking his head. 'I mean, she does her best considering what she has to put up with. Have you met her yet?'

Tim nodded, though he kept his mouth carefully closed. He knew that if he said anything about Molly, he'd start gushing - and if Crumcarey was anything like Brumeldsay - word would get back to her before he'd even finished his ice cream.

'Yeah,' he said at last when the silence had gone on a bit too long. 'She seems nice.'

'Ice cream, then?' said Stella.

'Yes please!' he said, glad to be back onto a safer subject. 'Do you have coffee flavour?'

'Of course!' said Stella. 'Fresh batch – prepare to have your tastebuds blown away. Frank's coffee ice cream is the best in the world.'

Tim dug the guidebook out of his pocket so that he could reach the coins underneath, and then spotted Frank eyeballing the book.

'You're not using that old thing to find your way around, are you?' he said with a laugh.

Tim grinned and shook his head. 'Nope. Honestly, I'm not even sure why I brought it with me.'

'Total rubbish,' said Stella, glancing over her shoulder for a peep. 'Those photos aren't even Crumcarey.'

'I know!' said Tim. 'They were all taken on Brumeldsay.'

'What makes you say that?' said Stella, holding out a cone towards him. It was heaped with enough ice cream to keep a family of five happy.

'Thanks!' said Tim, reaching up and taking it carefully. He gave it an eager lick and then let out a loud groan of delight. 'That's gorgeous.'

'Thanks!' said Frank with a pleased smile.

'And... I know it's Brumeldsay in the photos because I was born and brought up there. My mum still lives on the island - and I own a house just down the valley from her!'

'Wow!' laughed Stella. 'I mean, I can't say I've ever heard of it - but I bet my mum knows all about it.'

'Your mum?' said Tim, taking another massive lick of the ice cream.

'Yeah,' said Stella, nodding. 'Olive Martinelli. She owns the Tallyaff guesthouse. That's where you want to disappear to if the delights of the conference centre wear a bit too thin.'

'Oh cool!' said Tim. He'd seen the guesthouse through the minibus windows when Molly had picked them all up. 'I mean - I don't think I'm going to be decamping any time soon, though.'

'If you're saying that, I'm guessing you got the tower room?' chuckled Frank.

'Bingo!' said Tim. 'But don't tell the others how nice it is if you see them. I don't think Molly particularly fancies dealing with the fall-out if they find out!'

'Fair enough,' said Stella. 'But just so you know - mum does really good food, and I guarantee you'd be welcome. She's got the shop over there too... so... if you need anything...'

'I'll definitely visit before I leave,' he said, and then let out a long sigh. 'Right, I guess I'd better go and find a river... that may or may not exist.'

'That way!' said Stella, pointing out of the window towards a nearby field. 'It's not the great big torrent that book talks about, though. It's tiny. You can literally step right over it.'

'Thanks for the tip!' said Tim with a grin.

'Don't get lost in the woods!' said Frank, waving him off.

Tim gave the pair of them a salute.

Bonkers morning.

Bonkers place.

But at least it still wasn't raining.

CHAPTER 11

MOLLY

Molly couldn't remember a time she'd had to bite her tongue so many times in the space of one morning. They'd just arrived at the standing stones – and she'd already had enough of the professor's company. It had taken a lot longer to get there than usual. What would normally have been a brisk ten-minute walk had taken more than half an hour.

The professor had insisted on pausing every five seconds to point out potentially important landmarks as they went. First, there was the mound that could "represent a burial site." He was right… in a way. It was actually the final resting place of Mr Harris's ancient tractor.

Next came a large, flat stone with "significant" markings on it. The professor had practically wet himself with excitement as he'd pointed out the "possible Pictish runes" to the students.

This time – he was way off with his guess. The stone slab had actually been the base of a huge water trough. The markings he was so excited about were scratches that had happened during the high winds of storm Derek - about five years ago. The trough had toppled off its base, cracked in half, and then been carted away after Derek had got bored and wandered off to annoy Norway instead.

Now that they had reached the stones at long last, the waffle coming out of the man's mouth had gone from the sublime to the ridiculous… and Molly wasn't sure how much more she could take without biting clean through her lip.

'Now then,' he droned, 'these stones have stood here for centuries - battling the weather and the elements.'

Molly smirked and then did her best to tune him out. All she really wanted to do was head back to the castle and grab a cup of coffee before starting the unenviable job of making the students' beds. Unfortunately, Joyce's orders had been to stay put and remain at the professor's beck and call until he dismissed her.

'Get off my land!'

The shout made Molly spin on the spot - then she broke into a grin as the voice was joined by some fairly ineffectual barking. Trust Mr Harris and McGregor to turn up! The old man and his scruffy little dog never missed an opportunity to have a little fun when there were visitors around.

Molly liked Mr Harris a lot... but right now, she could really do without him scaring her guests. Just like she could really do without losing her job if she could help it - and she wouldn't put it past Mr Harris to regale the entire group with the full story of how the stones were erected.

Hurrying towards him, Molly waved Mr Harris down, desperate to stop him in his tracks before he reached the group.

'Molly, lass! I didn't see you there!' he said, beaming at her. 'I was just telling this lot to get off my land!'

'I heard!' she laughed. 'But... it's not your land... it's not *anyone's* land!'

That was the funny thing about Crumcarey. There were vast stretches of the island that basically belonged to no one - or everyone, depending on how you looked at it. The real owners of these plots had disappeared decades or even centuries ago – along with the paperwork.

'I know,' chuckled Mr Harris, lowering his voice, 'but it's fun to have a little shout at people every now and then, isn't it? Besides, I don't get the chance very often. I thought I'd better make the most of it!'

McGregor, who was busy sniffing Molly's wellington boots, growled and then let out a little bark as though he was agreeing with his master.

'So... what are this lot up to?' he said curiously,

nodding at the students who were all looking more than a little bit bored as the professor continued his diatribe.

'They're here to study the stones,' she said quietly. 'They're archaeologists.'

'They're idiots!' said Mr Harris stoutly, even as his eyes lit up with mischief. 'The stones are a hoax!'

'Shhh!' muttered Molly, putting a hand on Mr Harris's arm and dragging him a bit further away from the group. 'They'll hear you.'

'But… why does that matter?' he giggled. 'Surely it'll save them a bit of time.'

'Because Joyce will give me the sack if they find out!' said Molly, widening her eyes at him in a pleading fashion. 'She doesn't want their time saving.'

'Well, it's daft, that's for sure,' said Mr Harris. 'Why don't they do something useful - like looking into the sharks… or exploring the jellyfish?'

'I'll mention it to the professor when I get a second,' said Molly, shaking her head. 'Maybe he can pass the message on to the university. I think it might have to be a different department, though!'

'University,' huffed Mr Harris. 'What a waste of time. There's only three things worth learning about. Numbers, spelling, and sharks.'

'Not cows?' said Molly lightly.

Mr Harris shook his head. 'No point studying the cows. The only way you get to understand those hairy beasts is to work with them like me. You tell any of this lot - if they want to learn about cows, they can come and help me out for a few days. I'll teach them everything they need to know.'

'Will do!' said Molly, giving him a serious nod even as her cheeks started to ache with the effort. Why on earth a bunch of archaeology students would want to learn about cows was beyond her... but then, Mr Harris was quite... *interesting* at the best of times.

Right now, though, all she cared about was keeping him well away from her guests. As much as she'd already taken a disliking to the professor, she could really do without Mr Harris trying to scare him away from the site. She wouldn't put it past him - after all, the standing stones were McGregor's favourite spot for a walk.

'You're not going to let me talk to them, are you?' said Mr Harris, giving her a bushy frown.

Molly grinned at him and shook her head.

'Spoilsport,' he grumbled good-naturedly. 'Well, in that case, I guess we'd better find a different spot for McGregor to do his business.'

'See you soon,' said Molly cheerfully.

'Aye,' he said. 'Most likely you will. Bloody visitors.'

Molly kept an eye on him as he drifted off - limping along after McGregor as the little dog stuck his nose down every available rabbit hole as he went.

As soon as he was out of earshot, Molly breathed a sigh of relief. Disaster averted! If she hadn't been there to act as bodyguard, she had no doubt that Mr Harris would have had a wonderful time disabusing the professor of all his grand notions.

Taking a deep breath of increasingly damp air, Molly turned back to the little group who were all still gathered around the professor. Right… she guessed she'd better see if there was anything else they needed.

'Young lady,' grouched the professor the minute she reached them, 'I wish you would just leave us to do our work in peace. You're a hindrance rather than a help. I realise you don't know any better, but you could be standing on important, historical evidence and not even realise it. You simply do not have the training to be out here with us. If we need anything, we'll let you know.'

Molly knew a dismissal when she heard one.

For a moment, she just stared at him, fighting with the almost overwhelming desire to tell him just how *special* the stones really were. Oh, how she'd love to wipe that sanctimonious, smug look off his face. Instead, she forced herself to give him a sweet smile.

'Okay,' she said. 'I can do that.'

Molly gave them all a cheery wave and turned on her heel. It looked like she'd get that cup of coffee after all… and if she hurried, she might just about beat the rain. The clouds were definitely starting to converge overhead. She'd give it five minutes – maximum - before the heavens opened.

When she reached the edge of the field, Molly turned back for one last look at the group. The professor was busily taking an interest in the area around the base of one of the stones, dictating notes to the student with the blue topknot.

Molly chuckled, finally allowing a laugh to escape now that she was far enough away. That patch of grass was McGregor's favourite spot to have a wee.

Still laughing, Molly climbed over the gate and then paused for a second. She should really head straight back to the conference centre to make a start on tidying up after the students… but right now she was feeling a little bit… rebellious. In fact, she rather liked the idea of seeing if she could track down Tim instead. Hadn't he mentioned something about finding the river?

Molly stood for a moment, torn between being a good girl and giving Joyce the metaphorical middle finger for landing her with all this to deal with on her own.

'Alright, Mr Dimples,' she whispered, 'you win!'

Hunting down Tim definitely sounded like a lot more fun than discovering what sort of mess the students had made of their rooms!

CHAPTER 12

TIM

Tim stretched out on his grassy perch and let out a long yawn before popping the very last bite of his ice cream cone into his mouth. He grinned as he chewed. He'd be willing to bet pretty much anything the others hadn't enjoyed a second breakfast of ice cream! He'd done his best to make it last as long as humanly possible - but had then made the fatal mistake of biting off the bottom of the cornet – promptly dribbling coffee-flavoured ice cream right down the front of his coat.

Who cared though? There was no one to see him – and right now he was in his element. Fresh air and peace and quiet? He was practically in seventh heaven!

Wiping his fingers on his jeans to get rid of any remaining traces of ice cream, Tim opened the guidebook resting in his lap and flipped through the pages.

Thanks to Stella and Frank, he'd easily found his way to the stream.

If the book was to be believed – the river shouldn't be here at all. Instead, he should currently be sitting with his back propped up against a large oak tree - somewhere in the middle of an ancient forest.

The complete lack of trees here was the one thing Tim couldn't quite get used to. Brumeldsay was windswept and wild too - but it *did* have some of the most beautiful patches of ancient forest he'd ever seen – as documented by several photographs in the Crumcarey guidebook!

Tim searched through the pages until he found them again.

Crumcarey's ancient forests cover at least a third of the island.

'Erm… nope!' he laughed, glancing up from the page and staring around at the scenery. It was more like a windswept, coastal moorland than a forest.

Tim couldn't deny that Crumcarey was beautiful though – despite its lack of trees. The vast sky was marbled with storm clouds and the light was spectacular. Just like on Brumeldsay, the sun didn't climb too far above the horizon this early in the year. It simply peeped its head up, rolled along in a lazy arc and then disappeared to bed early.

The light was almost metallic - glittering golds,

bronzes and silvers splashed here and there - creating shimmering rainbows whenever the clouds decided they were carrying too much weight and dropped their burden on the fields below.

It was incredible to be on this island after hearing stories about it since he was a little boy. Even though he'd never set foot on Crumcarey before this trip, the place was almost a part of his DNA. He'd never dreamed he'd visit... especially not as an archaeology student with a job to do!

Not that he *really* had a job to do. Tim knew the professor had just made this task up simply to get rid of him while he focussed on the students who actually wanted to be archaeologists when they grew up. Tim was *already* grown up - not counting the dribble of ice cream down his front. He might be just a few years older than the others – but he'd bet he'd dealt with more than most of the rest of them put together. Not that he'd wish his experience on any of them.

Tim shuddered as the memory of his mum's pale face popped into his head. He'd spent so much time looking after her, it still seemed strange to be off doing his own thing... especially when what he was doing simply wasn't important.

After years of things being quite literally *life-or-death*, he sometimes had a hard time taking anything else too seriously. But... this was her wish. Tim had only gone off to university because of his mum... and her words drifted back to him with the tinkling of the water over the rocks at the bottom of the bank.

'You've got to live now, Tim. I'm better. Loads better. You've done your bit. Go grab yourself some life. Me and this old island aren't going anywhere - we'll be waiting for you when you want to come home.'

Giving himself a little shake, Tim did his best to swallow the lump in his throat. He might be having a hard time believing it – but his mum was fine - safely back on Brumeldsay and so much stronger than she'd been just a year ago when she'd finished treatment.

Blowing out a breath, Tim pocketed the book and hugged his knees to him, glad of his warm clothes. He wondered how the others were doing… and whether they were getting the chance to *"slowly and methodically unravel the complex intricacies of history and their relationships with it."* That was the line the professor kept on spouting – though as far as Tim could tell, they'd probably spend most of the morning investigating thistle patches and looking at piles of old farm scrap.

Peering back over his shoulder to check the weather hadn't crept up on him while he'd been enjoying his ice cream, Tim couldn't help but laugh. *He* might not be in danger of an imminent soaking, but things were definitely taking a turn for the worse over in the direction of the standing stones. The sky over there had turned a grumpy grey - with hints of black. It looked like the others were in for a drenching!

Something else besides the burgeoning rainclouds caught Tim's attention. Something much nearer to him. Lit by a shard of sunlight that was glancing down onto the winding track he'd just followed up from the road - was a person. It was impossible to tell who it was as they had their head bent against the swirling gusts of wind... but there was no doubt they were making their way towards him.

Oops!

Perhaps he'd better dig out his notepad and get busy looking like he was making some notes... even if he'd just spent the last twenty minutes or so doing little more than guzzling ice cream and admiring the view.

He pulled out the guidebook again and was just feeling around in his various pockets for his tatty notebook when he paused. He stared hard at the approaching figure for a long moment and then broke into a grin as he spotted a mane of long, dark hair swirling and tangling in the wind. It was Molly!

Doing his best to ignore the fact that his heart had just started hammering against his ribs like the tail of an overexcited Labrador who'd just heard the word "walkies" - Tim struggled to his feet.

'Hi!' he called, plastering what he very much hoped was a casual smile onto his face.

'Hey!' she said, returning his grin as she came

closer. 'Well... I don't need to ask what you've been up to!'

'Huh?' said Tim.

'You've got ice cream cone crumbs all down your front... and a dribble there,' she said, pointing at the front of his coat. 'Bet you bit off the bottom of your cone!'

Tim sniggered and nodded. He was more than happy to admit it. 'Premature nibbling – always been my problem!'

'Rookie error!' she laughed.

'I'm surprised you didn't pick one up on your way past,' said Tim.

'Trust me - I have to ration myself when it comes to Stella and Frank!' she said. 'Though – just for future reference, my favourite is the roasted strawberry and black pepper.'

'Noted!' said Tim, trying not to get too excited that she'd just used the word "future". 'So... what brings you all the way over here on such a gorgeous day?'

He glanced up at the patch of sky directly above them. It was brilliant blue, and for the moment the pair of them were bathed in golden sunshine. It was almost like magic.

'I thought you might have got lost,' said Molly with a grin. 'I asked Stella and Frank if they'd seen you and they pointed me up here. I think you gave them a bit of a surprise - they weren't expecting any customers today.'

'And I wasn't expecting to find an ice cream van!' said Tim, grabbing his guidebook out of his pocket and flipping it back open to the picture of a forest. 'Especially not in the middle of Upper Crum Woods.'

'Yeah,' laughed Molly. 'But then, to be fair, you're more likely to see an ice cream van than any trees around here. I hope you're not actually trying to get any sense out of that book?'

'I'll leave that up to the professor,' said Tim, shaking his head.

'Speaking of which, look!' she said, nodding for him to turn around.

Tim turned slowly on the spot as Molly pointed back in the direction of the standing stones. One dark blue-black cloud had just parked right above them, and by the look of the smudge of grey that extended down towards the ground... the others were busy getting a good soaking.

'Oops!' said Tim, turning to grin at Molly.

'Well... we'll just enjoy the sunshine, eh?' she said returning his smile. 'And the rainbows?'

Tim turned back only to find a great arc had appeared in the sky – extending right down to the ground on both ends. He'd never seen one so bright before.

'Magic!' said Molly, as a second appeared, almost as vibrant as the first, creating a perfect double rainbow.

'Not a bad place you've got here,' breathed Tim.

'Aye,' said Molly. 'Not bad at all.'

CHAPTER 13

MOLLY

'Back to that guidebook!' said Molly.

She had to break the silence somehow.

Tim was busy staring with childlike wonder at the stunning rainbow overhead - but she hadn't been able to keep her eyes off his face.

What was it about this scruffy guy that seemed to draw her attention like a magnet? Sure, he was gorgeous... but it was something more than that. He just exuded... joy?

Yes, that was probably the right word. There was something unabashedly *joyful* about the man. It didn't seem to matter to him that the professor had singled him out and sent him off to work on his own. Tim was more than happy. In fact, he seemed determined to make the most of every moment... and Molly found that irresistible!

In fact - she knew very well that she was in danger

of making a total fool out of herself if she wasn't careful.

'Guidebook?' said Tim, tearing his eyes away from the sky and turning back to her, looking slightly dazed.

'Just… don't believe any of the nonsense in it,' she said.

'I know,' said Tim.

'It's not even *about* this island,' she added. 'Not really, anyway! Apparently, the guy who wrote it and took the photos never even visited Crumcarey.

'I know,' said Tim again, starting to laugh.

'The descriptions are bonkers,' she said, ploughing on. 'I think the author just chose somewhere else he'd visited and changed all the place names.'

'Oh, that's definitely what he did,' said Tim, nodding.

'How'd you know?' she asked curiously. There was something in his tone that made her think he wasn't just agreeing with her to be polite.

'My dad wrote it!' he said with a shrug. 'And took the photos.'

Molly's jaw dropped, and she stared at him in open-mouthed surprise – verging on horror. Oh *great*. She'd just spent the last couple of minutes bashing Tim's dad? Suddenly, she wished she *did* have an ice cream – just to get rid of the taste of her own foot in her mouth!

'Sorry,' she muttered at last.

'Why?' laughed Tim. 'What you said is all true. The

photos were taken on Brumeldsay. Most of the descriptions are from there too!'

'That's… that's the island you lived on, right?' she said, suddenly feeling sheepish. He'd mentioned it the day before – but she'd been so flustered, she hadn't really been listening.

'Yes!' he said, beaming at her. 'Brumeldsay born and bred – that's me!'

'Cool,' she said, not really knowing what to say next.

Molly knew she should probably head back to the conference centre and leave Tim to it - especially now that she'd managed to insult his dad – but she'd look ridiculous if she turned tail two seconds after finding him!

'Erm… can you show me?' she said, nodding at the book.

Tim nodded, plopped down onto the bank of the little stream, and patted the tussock of grass next to him. Molly paused for a split second, and then with a shrug, dropped down next to him.

'May I?' said Tim, nodding at her lap.

Before Molly had the chance to figure out what he meant, Tim opened the book and laid it flat - half across his own lap and half across hers. She had to quickly rein in a little shiver of delight at the unexpected contact.

'See here,' said Tim, turning the pages until he paused at a big, double-page spread showing a wide, fast-flowing river surrounded by woodland. 'This is where we're meant to be sitting right now.'

'Seriously?' laughed Molly, glancing up from the book and staring around at the bare, windswept grassland that surrounded them.

'Yep!' said Tim. 'The house I grew up in is just out of shot to the left there - and my house now - the one I own - is just over the next hill!'

'You still own a place on Brumeldsay?' said Molly in surprise. 'I mean - you still live there?'

'Not at the moment,' said Tim. 'Mum still lives in my childhood home, and I settled as close to her as I could get. At the moment though, I'm in a student flat on the mainland - close to the university.'

'It must be exciting to get away from the island and explore a bit?' said Molly. She wasn't sure if she meant it, though. Sometimes she wished she had the nerve to cut ties with Crumcarey for a while and explore the world a bit more... she could really do with an adventure! Then the reality of leaving the island behind always stopped her from doing anything about it.

'Exciting? Kind of...' Tim said with a shrug. 'If I'm honest, it wasn't really *me* who wanted to move away.'

'What do you mean?' she asked, raising an eyebrow.

'Well...' he said, 'mum was desperate for me to get away from Brumeldsay for a while...'

'Oh!' said Molly, surprised. 'And you left just to please her?'

'It's not like you think!' he laughed, turning amused eyes on her. 'She was ill for a long time. Cancer.'

'I'm so sorry!' breathed Molly.

'Thanks. Just… one of those things, you know?' he said with a shrug. 'One of those *really shitty* things. Anyway – she's fine now. Loads better. But she's got this stupid thing where she thinks I stayed on the island just to look after her.'

'And *did* you?' said Molly gently.

'Not *just* to look after her,' he said, giving her a sheepish smile. 'But put it like this – there was no way I was even going to think about leaving until she was better or… or… better.'

Molly's heart squeezed at the forlorn look that briefly crossed his face. Without thinking about it, she reached out and covered his fingers with her own.

'I'm okay!' he said quickly.

Molly nodded, gave his hand a squeeze and then pulled away again, not wanting to make him feel uncomfortable. 'So… you went to university because she wanted you to… and joined this course, even though you wanted to study… geology, wasn't it?'

'Yep!' said Tim.

'Well, fair play to you,' she said, desperately casting around for something else to say. 'What about your house back on Brumeldsay?'

'I've got a friend staying there for now - just a kind of short-term set-up while he's doing some work on his own house.'

'Nice!' said Molly, staring down at the book again. 'I mean - the island looks lovely.'

'It is,' said Tim, looking a bit sad and wistful - a strange contrast to his usual cheeky grin.

'You know,' she said, deciding to change the subject back to the book, 'what I don't get is why there was such a mix-up. I mean, Alasdair Stewart – your dad - is a bit of legend around here… mainly for landing us with a completely useless guidebook. How does something like that even happen?'

'Well…' said Tim, cocking his head, 'mum told me he was on a deadline to get this whole series of books finished. He was already well behind schedule when he arrived on Brumeldsay – and he was running out of time to travel to the other destinations. Apparently, he had a habit of taking too much time doing the photos.'

'Wow!' said Molly. 'So… did your mum travel with him or…'

Tim shook his head. 'Nope. He met her when he arrived on Brumeldsay. He was meant to travel to Crumcarey next – so you could say I'm the real reason you guys got stuck with this mess!' he laughed, tapping the book with his hand.

'I don't get it…?' said Molly. 'I mean… I don't know when you were born… but surely this book is older than you?'

'Actually, we're about the same age… give or take about nine months,' said Tim with a wry smile. 'Dad turned up on Brumeldsay... and promptly fell for my mum.'

'Ohhh!' gasped Molly, as the pieces of the puzzle fell into place.

'Yep!' said Tim. 'He spent a bit more time on Brumeldsay than he was meant to – taking plenty of photos, and... erm... *exploring* the island with mum!'

'Blimey...' said Molly. 'That's quite some love story! So, did he settle down there?'

'Not exactly, no!' said Tim. 'He left about two weeks later than he was meant to - with enough photographs to complete not just the Brumeldsay guide, but to fake the Crumcarey one too. A month or two later, mum found out she was pregnant with me!'

'Tell me he went back to her when he found out?' said Molly, staring at him, wide-eyed.

Tim shook his head again. 'He was already married with three other kids. Obviously, mum didn't know that at the time – he only told her when she contacted him to tell him she was pregnant. She never saw him again. He did send her a signed copy of the Crumcarey guidebook when it came out, though. Nice of him, don't you think?'

'Nice?!' gasped Molly. 'What an... arse!'

She promptly clapped her hand over her mouth. That was Tim's dad she was talking about!

'Sorry!' she muttered.

'Don't be!' he said with a smile, flipping to the front of the book. 'Look – he even signed it for her!'

Molly glared down at the signature. He hadn't sent his love or asked how she was or left any kind of hint that she was anything to him other than a perfect stranger.

'I had to promise her I'd bring it back in one piece,' said Tim with a chuckle. 'It's got a certain amount of sentimental value.'

'I bet!' said Molly. 'I can't believe you're the son of the infamous Alasdair Stewart.'

'I know. Trust me - there are days I can't believe it either!' he said.

'Have you ever met him?'

'Nope,' said Tim, shaking his head. 'Never wanted to, either. Mum's the only family I've ever needed. Quite a good story though, eh? The son of the man who wrote a tourist guide without ever visiting the island!'

'I still can't believe he got away with that!' said Molly.

'Yep! Quite easily too, by the sound of it,' said Tim. 'I guess he knew no one was going to check up on him - at least in the short term. He just used different photos from the ones in the Brumeldsay book. That way he got to spend more time with my mum. Good thing too, I guess… otherwise I wouldn't even exist!'

CHAPTER 14

TIM

*L*eaning back onto his elbows, Tim stared up at the sky and wondered why he didn't feel more awkward. Molly was practically a stranger - they'd only set eyes on each other for the first time yesterday – but it felt like he'd known her forever. He'd never talked to anyone other than his mum about this stuff before - yet here he was, spilling his deepest, darkest secrets.

Tim's mum had always made sure that he didn't feel any kind of residual shame or embarrassment about the fact he'd never known his father. As a result - he didn't hold any kind of grudge against the man. He was a complete stranger – and over the years, he'd turned into a kind of comedy figure in their house – something they talked about when they were sitting around the log burner, telling silly stories. Tim would always be grateful to his mum for that.

Even so... this conversation had *definitely* strayed into much heavier territory than he'd intended.

'So,' he said, turning to Molly, determined to lighten the tone a bit, 'what's the real name of this stream - and where does it lead?'

'Well, we're obviously not sitting in Upper Crum woods!' she chuckled. 'This whole area - right down to the edge of the path where Stella and Frank are parked and back as far as the standing stones – is called the Links of Crum. It's kind of reverted to being common land these days... mainly because there aren't any records of who it really belongs to. Oh – and just FYI - don't listen to anyone who tries to move you on... especially not an old geezer with a scruffy little dog!'

'That's weirdly specific!' laughed Tim, raising his eyebrows.

'Yeah, well - Mr Harris and McGregor just paid a visit to your classmates. He's a lovely old guy really, but he does get bored now and then, and can't resist a bit of mischief.'

'Sounds like a character!' said Tim.

'You could say that,' laughed Molly. 'As for the stream... we've always called it the Wee Burn, but I'm not sure what its official name is. Its source is right up in the grounds of the conference centre – just behind the castle - and then it winds its way down here and all the way to the sea. Though to be fair, the sea is never that far away on Crumcarey!'

'Fair point,' said Tim. 'You're not having me on

though – are you?'

'About…?' said Molly, tilting her head.

'About the river being called the Wee Burn!' he sniggered, loving the fact that he was going to have to write that in the report for the professor later.

'Nope, not joking,' grinned Molly. 'It picks up a couple of other little trickles along the way - but never gets so big that you can't just step across it… if you're careful, that is.'

Tim laughed as he noted her not-so-subtle hint. Clearly, after almost plummeting backwards down the spiral staircase the previous day, Molly had the impression he was a complete clumsy idiot.

Maybe she had a bit of a point!

Just thinking about it again made him realise that he'd not actually had the chance to thank her properly. If it hadn't been for Molly's super-human reflexes, he'd probably be lying in a hospital bed back on the mainland right about now!

'Hey - Molly - I meant to say, thank you for saving me on the stairs yesterday,' he said, wincing slightly as he realised he sounded a bit like a wide-eyed idiot.

'It's fine!' she laughed. 'I've nearly done exactly the same thing so many times - it's a wonder I'm still in one piece. But… maybe I'd better keep an eye on you for a bit… just to make sure you don't get into any more trouble?'

Tim cocked his head and grinned at her. That had just gone *way* better than he had planned! Just the thought of having her company for a bit longer made him feel giddy, and it felt like a great big bubble of happiness was blooming in his chest.

What on earth was going on here?!

'Only if you haven't got anything better to be doing?' he said, trying to mask his excitement.

'I don't know about better!' said Molly with a shrug. 'I guess it depends if you think cleaning a bunch of mouldy portacabins and picking up after unwashed students counts as better?'

Tim wrinkled his nose and shook his head. 'Definitely not! What about your boss, though – won't she mind?'

'She told me I had to be ready to run around after the professor – whatever he wanted, apparently!' she said. 'Then the old git told me off because I might be trampling rare artefacts.'

'Now that I can believe!' snorted Tim.

'Yeah – well, never mind,' smirked Molly. 'At least it got me off the hook. Anyway – it means I'm not expected back up at work until the others go back. Seems like I've got some time on my hands.'

'It does, doesn't it?' said Tim with a broad grin. 'Tell you what - let's make the most of this sunshine while the others are getting drenched!'

'I like your style!' laughed Molly. 'So... what's your plan?'

'Why don't we follow the stream and see what we can find?' said Tim. 'I mean, I might as well do what the

FOOL'S GOLD ON CRUMCAREY

professor asked me to do. There's no point sitting around doing nothing all day - it's gorgeous out here, and I'd love to explore. If you're up for it?'

'Let's do it!' said Molly, scrambling to her feet and holding out her hand to him.

Tim stared up at her, doing his best not to get swept away by how beautiful she looked, framed against the golden sky with rainbows arcing overhead. He blinked and quickly grabbed her hand, letting her tug him to his feet.

'I've always loved this bit of the island,' said Molly, falling into step easily beside him. 'I haven't had a chance to walk here for a while.'

'Perfect excuse, then!' said Tim. 'I mean, I don't expect we'll find anything much... but hey – we might as well enjoy ourselves!'

'What exactly are we looking for?' asked Molly as they scrambled over the tussocky grass, following the little river upstream.

'Basically – anything man-made,' said Tim. 'Everything from stone walls, culverts and bridges to smaller items in the water.'

'Like what?' said Molly.

'Signs of life,' said Tim. 'Tools... pottery... jewellery...'

'Got it!' said Molly, training her eyes on the water and paying far more attention than Tim intended to give the job!

'So... what's Brumeldsay like?' she said after they'd

been walking for a few minutes in companionable silence.

'You just need to read the Crumcarey guidebook!' laughed Tim.

'No!' Molly giggled. 'I meant to grow up on!'

'I loved it. I still love it,' he said. 'I mean - peace, quiet, lovely community – what's not to love?'

'Ooh, look!' said Molly, coming to such an abrupt halt that Tim walked straight into her and had to grab her arm to stop her from toppling onto the grass.

'Sorry!' he gasped, as she laughed and did her best to get her feet back underneath her. 'What did you see?'

Molly pointed to the opposite bank. They both shifted closer to the water, peering hard.

'See it?' said Molly.

Tim nodded. It was the base of an old glass jar.

'Fish paste pot!' said Tim, scrambling down the bank so that he could lean across the trickle of cold, gurgling water to dig at it with his fingertips.

'There's no way you can tell that just from the bottom!' said Molly.

'Totally can,' he grunted, wiggling the pot as he did his best to work it out of the mud. 'I've been digging them up ever since I was a kid. They're practically indestructible. Ooh, this one's a beauty!'

Tim turned and held up the grubby glass jar so that Molly could see it. He always thought this particular design looked a little bit like a miniature glass hand grenade.

'That's actually quite cute!' said Molly.

'Right? I've always loved them,' said Tim, sloshing off as much of the mud as he could in the icy cold stream before holding it out to Molly. 'There - your first fish paste pot!'

'Don't you need to keep it for the professor?' she said with a raised eyebrow.

'Give over,' chuckled Tim. 'He'd definitely boot me off the course if I presented him with this.'

'Git,' said Molly in solidarity. 'Don't tell him I said that, will you?' she added quickly,

'Your secret is most definitely safe with me,' said Tim.

'Well it's his loss, anyway.' said Molly, pocketing the little jar. 'I love it.'

They continued to walk upstream, not finding anything more other than a broken fork and a piece of blue-glazed pottery.

'Definitely Ming dynasty,' said Tim, doing his best impression of the professor.

'More like... pre-Roman empire,' said Molly, scratching an imaginary beard.

'Aztec, I'd say,' said Tim holding it up to the light.

Molly giggled and Tim promptly decided it was probably his favourite sound in the world.

'What do you think it held?' she said.

'Goose pâte,' said Tim promptly.

'Really?' said Molly with a snort.

'Absolutely,' he said trying – and failing - to keep a

straight face. 'Did you know that it was the pâte favoured by woolly mammoths and sabre tooth tigers?'

'Now you're just making it up,' hooted Molly.

'You think?' said Tim, his voice deadpan. 'What gave it away?'

'Ooh look,' said Molly, 'there's another fork!'

This time, Tim watched as she pottered down the river bank and pulled half a broken fork out of the mud.

'Important find,' said Tim as she presented it to him.

'Yep, thought so,' said Molly. 'Probably from the Laird's castle.'

'Do you get the feeling we might be mixing our time periods up a bit here?' said Tim.

'Does it matter?' said Molly with a grin.

Tim shook his head and then peeped over his shoulder. 'Nothing matters really - other than making sure we keep ahead of that beast!' he said, nodding at a huge black cloud marching across the sky, intent on covering as much of the island as possible.

'We'll be okay for a while yet,' said Molly, giving it a quick look. 'It'll be chucking it down up at the stones by now though.'

'Oh dear,' said Tim, doing his best not to look too happy about that fact. 'The poor professor.'

'Yeah right,' laughed Molly. 'Once more with feeling, maybe?!'

CHAPTER 15

MOLLY

'Seriously, how long is this going to take?' huffed the professor. 'I've got to write up my notes – I haven't got time for this!'

Molly had to work really hard not to roll her eyes right in his face. She'd just had the most amazing time with Tim. Considering they'd only just met, they'd chatted easily about anything and everything. There had only been a handful of moments when they'd both gone quiet - and Tim had seemed to zone-out, staring intently at the river. Molly just figured he was thinking about his mum and had given him a second to come back to reality again.

Other than that, they hadn't stopped chatting, giggling – and just being plain silly – for the entire time they were together. If it hadn't been for the gigantic storm cloud putting an end to play – she would happily have spent the rest of the day exploring the Wee Burn with him.

As it was, the pair of them had had to sprint the final few meters to the conference centre – both of them play-fighting to get through the door first before the curtain of pelting rain reached them.

They'd bowled into the reception, panting and out of breath, only to find a dripping, shivering student waiting for them. Rhodri had barely managed to smile at her, his lips were that blue. Apparently, the professor had told him to wait for her to show up – and that the rest of the group was waiting for her in the Dining Hall.

After checking she didn't need a hand with anything, Tim had given her a little salute and disappeared through the door that would lead him up to his tower bedroom. She couldn't blame him. In fact, it had taken every ounce of her resolve not to leave the others to fend for themselves and follow him!

Sad to have to get straight back into work-mode after such a lovely morning, Molly had promptly rolled her sleeves up and followed Rhodri through to the Dining Hall, only to find a bedraggled hoard of young archaeology students and the professor all shivering in front of the burned-out fireplace. They'd left quite a puddle in front of the hearth – and not a single one of them had had the sense to get changed… or even grab a towel.

Taking pity on them, Molly ordered them all back

to their cabins to get changed - with strict instructions to meet her in the laundry room the minute they were ready.

Now – she had all three of the conference centre's beaten-up washing machines on the go – and the students were perched on plastic seats, watching as their muddy clothes went around and around in the brown, soapy water.

Going by the fact that most of them were wearing their pyjamas, Molly had a feeling that none of them had brought a decent, warm change of clothes with them. Even the professor had reappeared wearing a towelling robe instead of proper clothes. That might explain why he'd been trying to jump the queue from the moment he'd appeared with his armful of damp, filthy laundry!

'It'll be a while yet,' said Molly, trying to sound as patient as possible. 'Probably another twenty minutes on the wash… and we've only got the one tumble-dryer.'

'Ridiculous!' huffed the professor.

Molly just shrugged. 'You could always head back to your cabin for a while?' she said.

'And let this lot jump the queue? I don't think so!' he huffed.

Molly raised her eyebrows, noting the mutinous glares being thrown in his direction by the rest of the students. If he didn't watch out, *he'd* end up being the only sacrificial burial over at the standing stones!

An alarming clatter coming from one of the washing machines made Molly jump, and she winced as she stared at it in concern. It kept happening every couple of minutes as yet another stone freed itself from a pocket or turn-up. It was only a matter of time before one of the machines gave up the ghost.

Molly crossed her fingers in her pocket. Hopefully, that wouldn't happen. Getting a washing machine repaired on Crumcarey took some serious logistics… with a good number of prayers added in for good measure. For some reason, no one ever seemed to fancy the ferry trip out to them just to mend something as simple as a washing machine.

Of course – if the worst *did* happen, she could always beg Connor, the ferry captain, for help. He'd come to her rescue before. The guy was so used to keeping the island's knackered old ferry up and running that he had a knack for such things.

'Cheer up, you lot,' grunted the professor. 'It's just a bit of rain. We'll be straight back out there later!'

The students all groaned and slumped lower into their seats. Molly shot a glance at the professor. Sure enough – it was all just bravado. Even though the guy was well wrapped up in his dressing gown, he was shivering. Clearly that waxed cotton jacket of his had done very little to keep him dry in the storm.

The shivering didn't seem to stop him from spouting nonsense though – and any sympathy she might have for the man disappeared as he started to waffle on again, explaining why the stones they'd just spent the entire morning measuring and drawing in the pissing rain didn't match the ones in the book.

Molly focused all her attention on the washing machines. Maybe if she prayed hard enough, all three of them would make it out alive. The minute one of them came to the end of its cycle, she loaded up the tumble dryer - making sure the students' clothes got propriety.

'Right - I'm going to make everyone a round of hot drinks,' said Molly, desperate for any excuse to get out of the cabin for a moment. The smell of the half-dressed, unwashed, freezing students was one thing - but the waffle coming out of the professor was a whole new level of unbearable. 'Who wants tea and who wants coffee?'

She quickly made a mental tally as they all raised their hands, and was about to make a break for it when the professor called her back.

'Pop some brandy in mine too,' he said. 'Medicinal, of course. So that I don't catch a cold.'

Molly shook her head, doing her best to paste a polite smile on her face. 'Sorry, we don't have any.'

It wasn't entirely true... but the only brandy they had belonged to Joyce. There was no way Molly was about to head into her boss's private residence to search for it. She doubted Joyce's hospitality towards the man would extend as far as sharing her favourite tipple. Even if she was wrong - Molly knew from long experience that Joyce was pretty creative when it came to choosing hiding places for such things.

Molly watched as the old buffer's face fell.

'Well… ridiculous… ridiculous,' he muttered. 'Never mind, never mind – though I *will* be lodging a complaint.'

Molly shrugged and then promptly ducked out of the cabin before she started to giggle. The last thing she heard before dashing off to the kitchen was the professor telling the depressed, damp group that they'd better pull their socks up.

'Can't do that right now,' huffed one of the girls. 'My socks are in the wash.'

Molly snorted and dashed away before they could hear her laughing. The students might be a bunch of helpless kids… but she couldn't help but feel a bit sorry for them – stuck here with such a pompous pain the behind!

'I'll grab some extra blankets for them,' she muttered to herself as she flicked the switch on the three electric kettles, before turning to the ancient airing cupboard in the corner of the kitchen.

If the professor was really going to drag them back out into this storm, they'd need all the extra warmth they could get by the time they'd finished. No doubt the laundry room would be in for a second workout of the day too.

As the kettles came to the boil, Molly decided she'd better offer to drive the group back over to the Tallyaff first thing in the morning. They all needed at least one extra set of clothing to get them through their stay… at least, everyone apart from Tim did. It was either that, or they were going to blow up her washing machines and go down with pneumonia while they were at it!

Molly grinned as Tim's cheeky face popped into her head. She wondered what he was up to right now… maybe lounging around in his massive bathtub! She felt blood rush to her cheeks at the thought – and for the second time since they'd come back from their walk, she wished she could go up and join him and leave the rest of them to it…

'Focus, woman!' she huffed at herself. Her guests needed her. She wasn't getting paid to cavort around with the cute guy up in the tower bedroom!

Hoisting the heavy tray full of cups, Molly headed back towards the laundry room with a huge smile on her face. Frankly - she was more than happy to deal with the stroppy professor and a bunch of shivering students. It was worth it - just to have met Tim.

CHAPTER 16

TIM

It had been the best morning of his life.

'Don't be a blithering idiot!' Tim muttered to himself, doing his best to wipe the soppy smile off his face as he sat on the edge of his bed and began to unlace his muddy boots. The last thing he wanted to do was tread mud around the room and create more work for Molly.

'Molly...!' he sighed, and then promptly rolled his eyes at himself. When had he turned back into a soppy teenager?!

But... it *really had* been a lovely morning. Sure... there hadn't been anything particularly remarkable about the setting – but he'd had the best time wandering around with her. They'd spent hours spotting various bits of rubbish in the little stream and making up stories about it. It had been silly, and fun, and felt a lot like being six years old again.

Just the fact that he'd been able to talk to Molly about things he'd never been able to put into words before had been quite a surprise – but it had been just as incredible to discover how playful and unselfconscious she was too.

There had been moments when he'd seriously considered reaching out to take her hand. Luckily, common sense got the better of him each time – though it had been a close-run thing. Tim hadn't wanted to spoil anything - and the last thing he wanted was to make her feel uncomfortable. Just because *his* idiotic heart thumped with excitement every time she laughed, it didn't mean she felt the same!

Still - Tim had loved every second. They'd barely shut up the entire time they'd been out – other than to stop and stare in wide-eyed wonder at a rainbow now and then. Of course… there had been the couple of times Tim had found himself transfixed by something in the water too, but with any luck, Molly hadn't picked up on that!

In the course of the morning, Tim had gone from low-level dread about his time on Crumcarey to dreading having to leave the island. He knew he was being ridiculous – but it felt like he was in serious danger of falling for Molly Mackenzie… if he hadn't already!

After such an amazing morning, it had been quite a wrench to head back to the conference centre… but the weather had put a definite stop to play for a while!

FOOL'S GOLD ON CRUMCAREY

Tim had to admit, he felt a bit guilty about leaving Molly on her own to deal with the others. They really were a helpless bunch of babies... the professor included. He'd stopped briefly to see how they'd all got on over at the stones, but all he could get out of Rhodri was complaints. According to him, not only were they all soaked to the skin – they also had wet feet, blisters and insect bites.

Tim had never heard of midges being around this early in the year, but it looked like the field where the stones stood was some kind of winter vacationing spot for the bitey blighters. It must have been a wonderful surprise to be gifted a delicious bunch of unsuspecting archaeology students to feast on!

All in all, Tim wouldn't be surprised if the professor ended up with a full-blown mutiny on his hands if he wasn't careful! He had a feeling it would be even worse if the others found out what a great morning *he'd* had.

That wasn't the only reason Tim had made a break for it and hurtled back upstairs to his tower bedroom though. There had been something *other* than Molly's company that had sent his heart rate rocketing while they'd been exploring the banks of the river. Something he hadn't even mentioned to her... because if he was wrong, he'd look more than a little bit stupid.

Surely he was wrong. He had to be... didn't he?!

Tim didn't know much about the rock structures on Crumcarey. The castle was definitely built out of granite - he didn't need to go back outside to prove that - the walls were staring right back at him. But that didn't mean anything really, did it? The stones to build the castle could have been brought onto the island from elsewhere, even though it was fairly unlikely.

Still... he didn't think he'd been imagining those flecks he'd seen in the stream.

Well, there was only one way to find out if his hunch was right - and Tim was determined to do that the first chance he got. He needed to spend more time down at the Wee Burn... and to do that, he needed to play nice with the professor.

Kicking his boots under the bed so he didn't end up tripping over them later, Tim ambled over towards the large wooden desk. He had a plan.

As much as he'd prefer to spend the afternoon enjoying his lovely room and then ask Molly if he could take her out for a meal after she'd finished work... he was going to cosy up at this desk instead. He was going to confine himself to his posh tower room and craft a full report of his findings from the riverbank that would knock the professor's socks off.

Tim was fairly certain the grumpy git could be persuaded to jump at the chance of getting rid of him for the second day in a row. If he had a decent academic report that backed up his need to spend more time down at the Wee Burn... all the better!

'All right, Professor Estwick,' he sighed, slumping down at the desk and pulling his laptop towards him, 'let's get this work of fiction underway.'

CHAPTER 17

MOLLY

Molly climbed down from the knackered minibus with a sigh of relief. She sucked in a deep lungful of fresh, morning air before making her way around to the sliding door at the back to release the students.

It had been a decidedly smelly trip over from the conference centre to the Tallyaff. If her nose was to be believed - none of the guests had bothered with a shower. Not that she could blame them, of course - considering how disgusting the shower block was. No matter how much she scrubbed it – the old caravans never looked anything other than a mouldy hellhole.

Even so – the scent of unwashed bodies combined with the smell of wet dog that was wafting from the clothes that hadn't quite dried from the day before, meant Molly's nose remained wrinkled for the entire drive.

Despite an awful lot of grumbling – which included the word "pneumonia" being tossed around - Molly had kept her window open. If she was honest, she'd thought the students would be made of sterner stuff, considering they were in a profession that would mean they'd spend an awful lot of their lives outdoors!

As if the smell wasn't enough to drive her mad, the professor had chosen the seat right behind her – and he'd provided a soundtrack of pure nonsense all the way there. According to him, every single bump, mound and hill they passed would need investigating fully when he returned to the island for his next trip.

Molly knew that all this would be music to Joyce's ears, but to *her*, it had been a slow, painful kind of torture. Still, she'd kept her mouth shut and managed not to tell him that his possible "longship" was where an old stone barn had collapsed, and the potential burial cairn was where they'd enjoyed a Burns Night bonfire about fifteen years ago.

Of course, all this was made about a billionty-times worse by the fact that Tim had somehow snagged himself a seat with a direct line of sight to her rear-view mirror. As if it wasn't hard enough keeping a straight face with the professor spouting a constant stream of pure nonsense - every time he came up with a new clanger, she'd catch Tim's eye in the mirror. The quirk of his mouth nearly reduced her to tears with the effort of not laughing out loud - and those dimples of his distracted her so badly that it was a miracle they'd got there in one piece.

When the professor had announced that he was sure he'd just spotted the remains of a long-abandoned village, she'd had to turn her squeak of mirth into a hasty sneezing fit - and she'd very purposely avoided Tim's eyes for the rest of the trip.

'Right - everyone out!' she hollered as she slid the side door of the bus open. 'Olive should have everything you need to make yourselves a bit more comfortable for the rest of your stay!'

Molly stood back to let them all file out of the bus and make their way across the little car park towards the Tallyaff. She'd already called ahead to warn Olive that they were about to descend on her shop. She'd suggested her friend might like to get out her stash of hot water bottles, warm socks, coats, scarves... and any wet weather gear she had in stock. Olive had been thrilled at the potential influx of unexpected customers.

As for Molly - she was just looking forward to grabbing a coffee and a pastry with her friend while she waited for the others to max out their student overdrafts on all the things they really should have brought with them in the first place.

'You not heading in?' she said to Tim, as he hung back from the others.

'Oh... I will in a sec,' he laughed. 'I was just enjoying a hit of fresh air. The others smell a bit... ripe!'

Molly wrinkled her nose and nodded. 'Well, not everyone has the pleasure of a roll-top bath, you know!' she chuckled.

'That's true - but just for the record, I didn't smell as bad as that lot after a three-week camping trip where I hiked twenty kilometres every day!' laughed Tim. 'But… that's not to say I don't like the bath… because I definitely do! Very nice way to end the day, thanks very much.'

Molly nodded but didn't say anything… mainly because she couldn't trust her voice to behave itself while dealing with the very tantalising image of Tim in a bubble bath!

'Come on,' she said in a strangled croak as she nodded towards the door of the Tallyaff. 'Olive does seriously good coffee!'

'Fab,' said Tim. 'I might have a quick look around the shop too – there *is* something I'm after.'

Molly shrugged and led the way, still not trusting herself to meet his eye… just in case he could tell her imagination was still firmly up in his tower bathroom!

'Why'd you bring these trespassers in here?!' huffed Mr Harris as she made her way towards the bar, having pointed Tim towards the well-stocked shop.

'Oh hush, you!' laughed Molly.

She knew there wasn't any harm in the old man, but right now she wasn't interested in his version of banter. Molly was too keen to pump Olive for information about Brumeldsay. She really wanted to ask her friend what she knew about Alasdair Stewart too – but she'd need to do that without Tim overhearing… so it might have to wait for another day.

'Blimey,' laughed Olive, popping out from behind the bar to give Molly a brief hug. 'You weren't kidding when you said this lot didn't come prepared!'

'You think they look bad now?' said Molly in a low voice. 'You should have seen them after a day out in the rain yesterday. Drowned rats - the lot of them. Apart from Tim… but then he knows his way around our kind of weather!'

'Tim, eh?' said Olive, waggling her eyebrows.

'Not like that!' laughed Molly.

Not because it *wasn't* like that, but because she could really do without her friend cottoning on to her burgeoning crush. If Olive knew something, then so did the rest of the island. Considering Tim would be leaving in under a week - Molly could really do without the decade's worth of teasing that would follow!

'Anyway, what do you mean - he's used to our weather?' said Olive with interest. 'Has he been here before on holiday or something?'

'Nope,' said Molly, shaking her head. 'Apparently, he was brought up on Brumeldsay. Ever heard of it?'

'Of course I have!' said Olive. 'And you've seen a lot of it, even if you don't realise it. Those are the photos in the old guidebook!'

Molly raised her eyebrows and nodded with interest. So - Tim's story checked out. Not that she hadn't believed him, but hearing it from Olive suddenly made the whole thing a bit more real. But then… that meant the story about his dad was probably real too.

'So… you know Alasdair Stewart who wrote the book…?' said Molly.

'Of course,' chuckled Olive. 'Caused us plenty of nightmares with visitors coming over to check out our "enchanting ancient forests!"'

'Well,' said Molly, suddenly proud that she was in possession of a prime bit of gossip that she was pretty sure Olive hadn't heard yet, 'see that guy over there?'

'The tall one with the dimples?' said Olive, her eyes running up and down Tim, who was intent on scanning the shelves full of kitchenware for some reason.

'Yeah, him,' said Molly. 'That's Tim Stewart – Alasdair Stewart's son!'

'Well I never!' laughed Olive. 'What a strange coincidence.'

'Isn't it just?' said Molly. 'Especially as he wasn't even meant to be coming on this trip in the first place. Apparently, he was a last-minute replacement for someone who dropped out.'

Olive peered at Molly, cocking her head like an inquisitive spaniel before glancing back over at Tim again.

'What?' Molly demanded.

'I'm not so sure it's a coincidence after all,' said Olive slowly. 'Maybe… more like fate?'

'Oh hush!' laughed Molly. 'You and your romantic notions.'

'You should listen to her,' murmured Mr Harris. 'You know our Olive's never wrong.'

'I have no idea what you're talking about,' said Molly blandly.

'Well… here's a question for you then' said Olive.

Molly braced, fully expecting to get the third-degree about whether she fancied Tim, and if she did, what she was going to do about it.

'What?' she said cautiously.

'What I want to know,' said Olive, dropping her voice as the other students started to make their way towards them with baskets full of waterproofs and hot water bottles, 'is why this lot are buying survival kits, but young Mr Stewart over there seems to have picked himself out a wok!'

Molly frowned and glanced over at Tim. Sure enough, he was bringing up the rear of the little group, holding on tightly to a cast iron wok that had been on the shelf for ages. Years in fact. Molly was pretty sure it was the same one that had been there since she was a teenager – when a brief craze for Chinese cooking had swept the island.

What on earth?!

'Well, it's all sales to me!' said Olive with a shrug, before shifting over to the till.

Molly's eyes drifted sideways to the professor's basket. It looked like he had a bit of a different take on things when it came to making himself comfortable. Inside nestled not one, but two large bottles of brandy.

'Can we hurry things along!' he hollered, clearly in a hurry now that he had his hands on what he'd come for. 'I want to get back to the site and get on with it!'

Molly sighed. Bang went any chance of a pastry and a coffee with Olive. It was all aboard the conference express again!

'Don't worry, I'll put some pastries in a bag for you before you go!' hissed Olive. 'And maybe a clothes peg for your nose!'

CHAPTER 18

TIM

'Well, Mr Stewart, I have to say I'm impressed!'

Tim plastered what he hoped was a humble expression on his face as the professor waved his field report around in the air in front of him.

As soon as they arrived back at the conference centre from their short but decidedly useful trip to the Tallyaff, Tim had begged Molly for the use of her printer. He had a hunch he was more likely to read it if he was presented with a physical copy rather than an email attachment… and he'd been right.

Tim knew he couldn't take all the credit for the professor's new, rather improved mood though. He had a feeling it might have something to do with the faint waft of brandy that was coming off him. Not that he cared. If it meant the miserable old git let him slip off to the stream again, he was happy!.

'Thank you, Professor Estwick,' he said, keeping his voice dead serious... with a slight hint of *suck-up* thrown in for good measure.

'Credit where credit's due, old boy!' said the professor, waving the pages around again. 'It's a nice job.'

Tim smiled and did his best to ignore the brandy-soaked condescension wafting his way. Of *course* the professor liked it. He'd made sure that it contained all hi favourite words.

Artefact. Situation. Contextualisation. Juxtaposition.

He'd waffled for pages about the significance of anything and everything and then had finished off with an entire section on why it all needed further careful investigation.

'You know,' said the professor, weaving slightly, 'we might make an archaeologist out of you yet.'

Tim raised an eyebrow.

'Well... it *is* incomplete,' he said quickly - just to make sure he'd hammered the point home properly. 'I was wondering... I know it's a lot to ask... but maybe you'd be kind enough to spare me again today so that I can finish it up for you?'

Tim paused and watched as the cogs started to turn behind the professor's eyes. It looked painful!

'I mean,' he added, 'while the others with more experience continue their work at the standing stones.'

Tim paused again, wondering if he'd managed to hit the mark yet. It was impossible to tell from the slightly glazed look on the professor's face.

'It's a fine idea,' said the professor at last, his head bobbing up and down like a nodding dog. 'A very fine idea - keep up the good work, Tom.'

'It's Tim,' sighed Tim. 'And thanks, I'll do my best!'

Turning away from the professor, he broke into a wide smile. He really wanted to let out a few fist-pumps in celebration - but he had a feeling the old git might notice that - no matter how much brandy he'd poured down his neck!

This was just what Tim had been hoping for. Now he could head back to the stream and test out that hunch of his. It might turn out to be nothing, of course… but his gut was telling him that he'd spotted something yesterday that might end up being far more significant than a bunch of stones piled up in a field by a farmer!

Not that he'd breathed a word about it in his report, of course!

Making his way across the hall, Tim ducked through the low doorway and headed back towards the reception. He wanted to put as much distance as possible between himself and the professor before he had a chance to change his mind.

His plan was to nip up to his room, grab the wok, and then head straight back to the river. He was just debating whether to ask Molly if she fancied coming along for another adventure when he entered the reception, only to find the woman in question surrounded by a gaggle of his classmates.

'It's my bra!' screeched Lucy.

'Mine!' howled Jo.

'As if!' growled Rosie. 'You don't even wear one!'

Tim bit his lip, trying not to laugh as he saw Molly roll her eyes in pure exasperation. She was holding what looked to be a basket of laundry that clearly hadn't been reunited with its owners the previous day.

Catching her eye, Tim shot her a wink. Molly grinned at him before turning back to the others and placing herself bodily between the three girls as they started to yank at the bra like a bunch of puppies with a chew toy.

Tim rolled his eyes and made a break for it – heading across the reception and through the doorway that led up to the tower. So much for asking Molly to join him. He couldn't risk the others hearing what he was up to – and he didn't want to have to wait until they cleared off.

Tim was anxious to get started. It was a pleasant morning out there right now - but he couldn't risk the weather changing. If they had another downpour, the water in the Wee Burn would rise and that would put an end to his little experiment before it had even started.

Two minutes later, after risking life and limb by taking the spiral staircase at a run both on the way up and then back down again, Tim reappeared in the reception with his new wok tucked under one arm.

The girls were still fighting over the basket of

lingerie, but as he made his way across the room, they all turned to stare at him. Tim ignored them as they nudged each other, laughing as they spotted the heavy pan he was carrying. It was clear they all thought he was a bit of an idiot – but frankly, he didn't give two hoots.

With one last regretful glance over his shoulder at Molly, Tim made a break for it.

CHAPTER 19

MOLLY

It had taken her an age to get away from the squabbling students. Okay... well... maybe not really an age - but that's what it had felt like. In the end, she'd just plonked the basket on the floor between them and let them have-at-it like a bunch of hyenas.

Molly didn't care. She was more interested in what Tim was up to. She'd got the feeling he'd wanted to say something before heading outside – though she couldn't blame him for not hanging around, what with the warring wild animals she'd been doing her best to hold at bay.

What she *hadn't* understood was why he seemed to be taking his new wok for a walk!

Closing the door on the shrieking students, Molly paused to wind her scarf tightly around her neck. She had a hunch Tim was heading back over to the stream.

With any luck, he wouldn't mind if she joined him again. She had a feeling he'd wanted to ask her – but hadn't dared to with the other students around.

Considering the pair of them had only met just a couple of days ago, Molly found herself weirdly drawn to Tim Stewart. It was like her entire being was aware of him all the time.

'You're an idiot, Molly Mackenzie!' she muttered. 'He's a guest, and you know what you're meant to do with guests, right?'

The wind answered her by kissing her on the cheek and she shook her head quickly.

'Wrong answer! We don't kiss them… we keep our distance!'

Molly let out a long sigh and started to make her way down the gravel driveway towards the road. No matter what silly ideas she was getting about Tim, the reality was that he was only there for a few more days and then he'd be off - doing the rest of his course, or heading back to Brumeldsay to see his mother… or whatever else he decided to do with his life. And her? She'd be on Crumcarey - wishing things could be different - desperate for an adventure she'd never be brave enough to grab.

Molly shook herself. This was a dangerous road to be going down. She loved her island home… but she had to admit that her life had become too small for her liking. Her parents had moved to the mainland a few years ago, and most of her friends moved away too. They were all busy with careers, babies, getting married or travelling the world.

Molly had stayed put on Crumcarey because she loved island life... and she'd really believed Joyce was going to do something special with the conference centre. She'd been excited to be a part of it.

Sadly, the truth of the matter was that Joyce was slowly leaching the life out of the place... and Molly too while she was at it. No matter what Molly did to keep the old place together and make the best of things – knowing that it wasn't in her power to turn the business around was heartbreaking. She'd just about had enough of watching something she loved fall apart because of someone else's indifference.

Molly had just reached the end of the driveway and was busy raking the horizon for any sight of Tim when she heard someone calling her name. Her heart sank. She'd come so close to making a break for it!

Turning quickly, she spotted Joyce hurrying towards her.

'Why is there someone walking around with a saucepan?' said Joyce.

No preamble, no check-in. Typical Joyce!

'It's a wok, not a saucepan,' said Molly with a small smile.

'Well... that's not the point,' huffed Joyce. 'Answer the question!'

'Honestly, I have no idea,' said Molly with a shrug.

It wasn't a lie, after all. Plus, she didn't want Joyce to get wind of the fact that she'd spent any more time with Tim than the others.

'Well - I want it back,' said Joyce, looking more than a little putout. 'Guests are *not* welcome to help themselves to things from my kitchen!'

'Oh,' said Molly, 'you don't need to worry about that. He bought it from the Tallyaff this morning.'

'What?' said Joyce in surprise. 'Why?'

'I've got absolutely no clue,' laughed Molly.

'But… why does Olive have woks for sale, of all things?' said Joyce, looking even more confused.

'Well… she doesn't. Not anymore, at least,' said Molly. 'That was the last one. I think it's been there since I was a kid… there was a craze for Chinese cooking for about a week. I remember everyone trying to get their hands on duck breast!'

'Right… okay…' said Joyce, her eyes darting about as though she was on the lookout for any more guests bearing items of unexpected cookware. 'You know, I think some people lose the plot a bit when they arrive on Crumcarey.'

Molly had to bite back a smile. Joyce was a prime example of someone arriving on Crumcarey and losing their grip on reality… not that she'd spot the irony of her statement, of course!

'Was there anything else?' said Molly lightly. She

really wanted to follow Tim and see what he was up to, but there was no way she wanted Joyce to get wind of the fact that she wasn't exactly making herself indispensable to the professor like she'd been told to.

'Nope,' said Joyce. 'As long as no one's helping themselves from the kitchen, who am I to dictate.'

'Well, quite!' said Molly.

'You know - I think people have to be a bit mad to come here in the first place,' said Joyce, rolling up one jumper sleeve before unrolling the other. 'Some of the things that go on during the wine festival are pretty strange too. Like that one time-'

'You know,' said Molly, interrupting, 'I think I'd better hurry off and make sure the - er - the group have everything they need?'

Joyce stared at her for a moment and then nodded.

'Okay. Fine. See if you can find out what that young man is up to with his wok,' she said.

'I'm on it!' said Molly with a grin.

How unexpectedly perfect? Joyce had literally just given her permission to follow Tim. Maybe the universe was conspiring in her favour for a change!

Molly watched as Joyce drifted off in the direction of the laundry room. Goodness knows what she'd get up to in there. No doubt she'd leave some kind of mess for Molly to sort out later… but if it kept her boss busy and out of the way long enough for her to make a break for it, Molly didn't really care right now!

The minute Joyce disappeared inside, Molly turned and began to route-march in the direction of the Wee Burn. As soon as she rounded a bend in the road that meant she was out of sight of any prying eyes, she picked up her pace even further – breaking into a kind of half-jog, half-skip as she pelted along the road.

It took a full five minutes before Molly spotted her prey in the distance - and another five minutes to actually catch up with him. The man was walking ridiculously fast – and he was clearly on some kind of mission.

'Hi!' he called, turning around having clearly heard her approaching at a gallop.

'H-H-hey!' she puffed, drawing to a stop, completely out of breath.

Molly knew she must look a right state… but she didn't care right now. She was too curious to find out what Tim might be up to worry about such piddling things as being bright pink in the face. The fact that her hair was probably sticking up where the wind had done its best to undo her plait didn't even factor into the equation!

'Hi!' he said again, laughing. 'You okay?'

Molly bent over, grabbed her knees and did her best to get her breath back. Then – realising she couldn't quite get any more words out just yet - she looked up and gave him the thumbs up.

'Is there an emergency? Or…' Tim petered off, still looking mildly amused though there was a definite hint of concern in his voice.

'No!' puffed Molly. 'Everything's fine.' She was starting to feel a bit daft... but hey, she'd come this far, so she figured she might as well get to the bottom of the mystery. 'I was just wondering what you're up to,' she added. 'You know, with the...'

She gestured at the wok, and in return received a full-wattage grin - complete with the reappearance of those dimples - which did absolutely nothing for her heart rate.

'I'm... testing a theory,' said Tim at last.

'A theory?' she said in confusion, straightening up.

'Right!' said Tim with a nod.

'With a wok?' she said.

'Uh-huh,' he said, setting off again – this time at a gentler pace - and gesturing for her to follow.

'What sort of theory?' said Molly, falling into step beside him.

'A very interesting theory!' he said with a cryptic smile, before spearing sideways off the road so that they could begin the scramble over the tussocky grass towards the same patch of bank they'd been sitting on the day before.

As soon as they reached the spot, Tim dropped the wok into the grass. Then, much to Molly's surprise, he started to unlace his walking boots.

'What are you up to now?!' she laughed.

'I'm going to take my shoes and socks off and go for a paddle!' said Tim calmly, as though this was perfectly normal behaviour to be engaging in in the middle of winter on a windswept island.

'Why on earth would you want to do that?' squeaked Molly.

Just the thought of the bitterly cold water made her curl her toes up inside her lovely warm boots.

'It's… an experiment!' said Tim. 'Going to stick around to watch?'

Molly nodded. After all, she'd come this far… she might as well watch Tim undress….

Not that stripping off a pair of socks counted as undressing...

Shame it was just socks really...

Still, it was better than nothing! Besides, if she was lucky he might roll his trousers up and then...

Yay!

As though he'd been reading her mind, Tim started to roll up one of his trouser legs, revealing a long stretch of muscular calf.

Molly swallowed.

Still, he was bound to squeal like a pig when he got into the cold water… at least that would undo the spell a bit!

Tim steadied himself with one hand on the tufty grass as he eased his way down the bank, his wok held tightly in his other hand. When he reached the bottom, he stepped into the icy water without even the slightest shudder.

Impressive!

Molly licked her lips and flopped down onto the bank to watch. So much for the spell being broken – she couldn't tear her eyes away from Tim Stewart even if she wanted to!

CHAPTER 20

TIM

*D*ipping the wok into the freezing stream, Tim scooped up some of the rock and sediment from the bottom along with a good slosh of water.

'What on earth are you up to?' chuckled Molly from her spot on the bank.

Tim grinned up at her briefly but didn't answer. Instead, he plonked his bum down onto a nearby boulder and started to swish the gravel around, lowering it every now and then to carefully slosh some of the murk away and add fresh water.

'Wait… you're panning for gold?!' laughed Molly.

'Yup!' said Tim, not taking his eyes off his bowl.

'Here?' said Molly.

'Right here,' agreed Tim, scooping up a little more water.

'You've got to be kidding me?' giggled Molly.

'Nope - not kidding,' said Tim.

He knew he probably looked like a total lunatic right now, but he wasn't too bothered. After their adventure together the previous day - and the ridiculous stories they'd made up about everything they found - Tim knew that Molly probably thought he was just mucking around again.

He wasn't though. Not this time. He was deadly serious.

'I could be wrong, of course,' he said fairly.

'But you don't think you are?' said Molly in surprise.

'I don't think I am!' agreed Tim.

He continued, steadily swishing and emptying, swishing and emptying, throwing the larger stones back into the river as he went. At long last he paused and carefully inspected what was left in the bottom of the wok.

'Anything?' asked Molly curiously.

'Nah,' said Tim. 'Not yet!'

He quickly started the same process again – aware of Molly's eyes on him the whole time.

'What about now?' she said when he paused again.

'Nope,' laughed Tim.

'My turn, then!' said Molly.

Tim raised his eyebrows and peered across the little stream in her direction, only to find Molly eagerly stripping off her shoes and socks. Suddenly, Tim's focus dissolved as he stared at a tantalising glimpse of bare ankle as she lowered herself into the icy water.

'Okay,' said Tim. 'I'm officially impressed. You didn't even flinch!'

'Give over!' said Molly, rolling her eyes at him good-naturedly. 'I've been paddling around in Crumcarey's streams and sea since I was just a wee girl.'

Tim held his hand out for her to grab hold of to steady herself as she came to stand next to him.

'Alright,' she said, 'let me at it!'

Tim handed her the wok.

'Erm...' she laughed, 'you might need to tell me what to do!'

'Okay,' said Tim, moving to stand behind her. He was just about to reach around either side of her so that he could guide her hands, when he paused. 'Do you mind if I show you?'

'Of course!' she said, grinning at him over her shoulder.

Tim felt something in his chest give a hopeful flutter. What was it about this woman?! She seemed to be waking something in him that had been asleep since before his mum got sick.

'Right,' he said, doing his best to focus on the job in hand rather than the warm body that was happily settling back against him as he reached around her to grip the wok and guide her movements. 'So... you scoop up a bunch from the bottom, then you kind of do this...'

He started to shift the wok so that Molly could get a feel for it, all the while doing his best to remember that he was trying to teach her - not cuddle her. The fresh scent of strawberry coming from her hair wasn't doing anything to help matters!

'Like this?' said Molly.

'Exactly,' said Tim, gently letting go so that she could take over – all the while cursing that she was such a quick learner!

Shifting out of the way so that Molly had more room to work, Tim went to sit on the bank to watch. He kept his feet in the water - they were starting to get a bit numb, but he'd not felt so alive in ages.

He smiled as he watched Molly. She was concentrating so hard that a little line had appeared between her eyebrows, and her tongue was poking out between her lips as she washed and swished, washed and swished – examining the bottom of the wok as though her life depended on it.

What if he was wrong? He'd look like a right lemon! Maybe he should just have stuck to looking for fish paste pots and knackered old bits of cutlery instead.

'How are you doing?' he said, watching as Molly paused to stare into the wok again. She was clearly getting down to the last tiny fragments of her first try.

'Come have a look!' she said.

Tim stood up and sloshed back across the stream to where she was perched on the boulder.

'Wow - you've done a much nicer job than me!'

laughed Tim, looking down at the fine, dark gravel in the bottom of the pan. Molly angled the wok slightly – turning it this way and that.

'Wait!' said Tim, as a ray of sunlight glinted off something hiding in the sludge.

'There!' said Molly.

They'd both spotted it at the same time – a tiny grain of something bright… no bigger than a sesame seed.

'There's another,' gasped Molly.

'And there!' said Tim, pointing at a third spot.

'Oh. My. Goodness! said Molly, glancing up at him with wide eyes. 'Gold?'

'Gold!' Tim nodded. 'At least… I think it is.' He couldn't believe his hunch had been right.

'Will you take this from me before I drop it?' said Molly, sounding a bit like she was trying to hold her breath - as though speaking or even breathing anywhere near the wok might make the tiny grains they'd spotted disappear.

Tim took pity on her and took the heavy wok carefully out of her hands. Stretching up to the top of the bank, he rested it carefully in the grass.

'My feet have gone numb!' laughed Molly, trying and failing to get up from the boulder.

Tim reached out a hand and pulled her to her feet. Then, without even thinking about it, he gently pushed a loose strand of dark, strawberry-scented hair back behind her ear.

'You just found gold on Crumcarey!' he said, his eyes wide as he held her steady.

'*We* just found gold on Crumcarey,' she amended in a whisper. And then, before Tim could even guess what was going to happen next, Molly flung her arms around his neck and kissed him.

CHAPTER 21

MOLLY

Tim's lips were so warm that Molly nearly groaned with delight. Her feet might be so cold they were practically numb, but the rest of her hadn't got the message about getting out of the freezing water - she was too busy kissing this man as if her life depended on it.

'Sorry!' she gasped, suddenly coming to her senses and pulling away. She'd just launched herself bodily at one of the conference centre guests!

'I'm not!' grinned Tim.

Molly stared at him for a long moment… and then relaxed. This was Tim - the guy she'd joined on a mattress to test its bouncy-score. He was the man who'd told her how hard it had been to care for his mother during her cancer treatment – at times not knowing whether she'd still be with him in the morning. They'd told each other stories about their island homes – the good *and* the bad. He was Tim… the man she'd just struck gold with.

'Okay… sorry-not-sorry!' she said, breaking into a grin and leaning forward to plant the smallest, softest kiss on the corner of his mouth. 'Come on - let's get up on the bank. My feet need to un-freeze!'

Tim smiled at her before leading the way out of the water, offering her his hand and pulling her up behind him - which was just as well considering she *really* couldn't feel her toes by this point. Molly had a feeling she was in for the world's worst bout of pins and needles when she warmed up a bit!

'Well… we weren't seeing things,' she said, slumping down into the grass and peering into the wok again. If anything, there were even more glimmers of gold in there than they'd noticed before. 'Is it definitely gold? Not that fool's gold stuff?'

'Pyrites?' said Tim, settling down on the bank so that the wok sat between them. 'I mean… it could be.'

'But you don't think so?' said Molly.

Tim shook his head. 'See how these bits are kind of rounded? Pyrites tends to be more angular – you can see the crystals more, if that makes sense.'

'A bit hard to tell though – these bits are pretty small – apart from that one there… it's about the size of a grain of rice!' said Molly, excitement rising in her. 'That definitely looks quite curvy!'

'If only I had a bit of copper!' said Tim, running his fingers through his hair and staring around distractedly as though he might find some just sitting in the grass.

'Why?' laughed Molly.

'Well... gold has a Mohs hardness of two and a half, but pyrites is more like six to six and a half. Copper has a hardness of three.'

'O-kay?' said Molly, trying to keep up. It looked like she'd just discovered where Tim's particular freak flag lay!

'So – gold won't scratch copper, but pyrites will - because it's harder,' said Tim.

'Oh!' said Molly. 'I get it. So... rocks and stuff?'

'Kinda my thing!' chuckled Tim.

'That's cool,' she said with a smile. 'Anyway - try it on this!'

Molly shook back the sleeve of her jumper to reveal the wide copper bracelet she always wore.

'Perfect!' gasped Tim. 'I mean... as long as you don't mind? If it *is* pyrites, it'll leave a mark.'

'Just do it on the inside!' said Molly, slipping it off her wrist and handing it over.

Tim took it and then paused, staring down into the wok.

'What are you waiting for?' demanded Molly.

'It's pretty small... I'm bound to drop it,' said Tim.

'I've got a napkin in my pocket from the pastries Olive slipped me earlier!' said Molly, taking it out and shaking out the crumbs before handing it over. 'Do it over that – at least it'll stop it from disappearing into the grass!'

Molly held her breath while there were several false starts as Tim struggled to get a grip on the tiny, glimmering grain. At last, he managed to draw it across the smooth inside of Molly's bracelet while she held it still for him.

'And?' she said, her voice practically quivering with excitement.

'No marks,' said Tim, peering closely at the copper. 'And I managed to do that quite hard, too!'

'So…'

'So… I think it *is* gold!' said Tim.

'Okay… wow!' squeaked Molly, staring at him in wonder.

'I want another go - don't you?' said Tim, glancing back down into the wok with wide eyes and then back at her again.

Molly nodded, beaming at him. 'I *definitely* want another go,' she said, though she wasn't sure if she was talking about panning for gold or snogging his face off.

Maybe a bit of both!

'Cool!' said Tim. 'We'll just scoop the rest of this onto the napkin. We can fold it into the middle and search through it properly when we get back to the castle – it'll be easier up there!'

'I'll grab a couple of stones to weigh the edges down in case we find any more,' said Molly.

'Good thinking!' said Tim.

They took it in turns with the wok, and it was a bit like they'd broken the seal - both when it came to finding gold - and kissing!

'Alright!' said Tim, pulling back from her and getting to his feet after what felt like hours perching next to her on the boulder. 'I'm going to be the grown-up for a second and call time. I think I've got ice cream freeze in my feet from the water!'

'I don't know what you're complaining about!' laughed Molly, clambering to her feet and following him to the edge of the stream. 'I've not been able to feel my feet at all for at least twenty minutes now!'

Between them, they scrambled back to the top of the bank one last time - a feat that had become harder and harder to do the colder they got.

'Socks and shoes time!' declared Tim.

'Aww!' laughed Molly, though it was definitely a half-hearted complaint. She was now cold to the core and desperate for a bit of a walk to warm up.

'You know,' said Tim, glancing across at her, 'I think we need to have a serious talk.'

Molly frowned, noticing his dimples were suddenly missing in action. That didn't bode well! As for a serious talk… wasn't it a bit soon for that? After all… they'd just kissed. Nothing else. So far, at least!

'Why are you looking so worried?' chuckled Tim, lacing up one of his boots.

'Erm… serious talk?' said Molly.

'About what we just found!' said Tim. 'I mean… we need to tell someone about it… but who?!'

'Oh!' said Molly, feeling her heart bob with relief. 'Well… definitely not Joyce!'

'Really?' said Tim. 'She was my first thought…'

'Nope!' said Molly. 'Like I said - the land doesn't belong to her, and I can guarantee she'd make a pig's ear out of the whole thing somehow.'

'Fair enough,' said Tim.

'What about the professor?' said Molly.

'Nope. No way!' said Tim, shaking his head with a finality that made Molly laugh out loud. 'That idiot?! He'd wrap the entire thing up in academic waffle. Seriously - there'd be appraisals and assessments, and he'd somehow find a way to make it all about him because he's leading this merry band of losers.'

'Come on Tim,' said Molly with a smirk. 'Tell me what you really think!'

'Plus…' said Tim, who was clearly not quite finished, 'he'd conveniently forget we were the ones who found the gold in the first place!'

'I don't mind that so much,' said Molly with a shrug.

'Well… actually, me neither,' said Tim. 'But I still think he'd be a complete nightmare!'

Molly nodded as she did her best to yank her socks on over her still-damp feet.

'Here!' chuckled Tim, stealing the socks from her. 'Allow me.'

'You're seriously going to put my socks on for me right now?'

'Got a problem with that?' said Tim, wiggling his eyebrows at her.

'Are you kidding me?' laughed Molly. 'Be my guest!'

Tim rolled the socks up, then grabbed one of her bare, frozen feet and pulled it onto his lap. Instead of pulling the sock straight on for her, he started to rub it vigorously.

'Oh my g... stop stop stop!' laughed Molly, squirming around and doing her best to get her foot out of his grasp.

'What?' said Tim. 'Don't tell me you're ticklish?'

'Nope!' said Molly, still giggling, 'but I've got pins and needles. It feels like you're tattooing my entire foot in one go!'

'Oh!' laughed Tim. 'Well... you know the best way to get rid of that?'

'What?' said Molly, unable to think straight with her foot still resting in his warm hands.

'Rub harder!' he said, doing just that.

Molly squealed as the blood rushed back to her frozen toes.

'There!' he chuckled, quickly rolling one sock on before giving her other foot the same treatment.

This time, Molly didn't put up a fight - mainly because he was right. Her feet were warming up nicely... and besides, how often did a gorgeous man offer to put her socks on for her?

'Hey Molly?' said Tim, as she reluctantly extracted herself from his lap to pull on her own boots.

'Mmm?' she said.

'How would you know what it feels like to have a tattoo?'

Molly glanced across at him and gave him a wicked wink. 'Wouldn't you like to know?'

'I totally would, actually,' he said. 'Have you got one?'

'Yup.'

'Where?' said Tim.

Molly could hear the curiosity in his voice.

'That's for me to know, and you to find out… maybe… if you're lucky!' she said, wiggling her eyebrows at him.

'Sounds like a challenge!' he said.

Molly grinned and focussed back on her laces. 'What about you?' she said. 'Any tats?'

'Are you kidding me?' he laughed. 'My mum would have had a fit!'

'Mine too - if she ever found out,' said Molly.

'Doesn't she know?'

Molly shook her head. Her tattoo *definitely* wasn't somewhere her mum would spot it by mistake, but there was no way she was going to tell Tim that - it would totally give the game away!

'What I want to know,' said Tim, 'is where you found a tattoo artist on Crumcarey?'

'I didn't,' laughed Molly. 'I went to Edinburgh with

some friends for my eighteenth. Got it done while I was there.'

'Well... that makes more sense!' he chuckled. 'I somehow can't imagine a tattoo parlour getting enough customers to keep them going up here. I mean... maybe Mr Harris...'

Molly let out a hoot of laughter. 'Oh, I'm sure he's got one or two hiding underneath those moth-eaten jumpers of his!'

'Doesn't bear thinking about,' laughed Tim. 'Actually... getting off the subject of tattoos for a minute... is that who we should tell? About the gold, I mean?'

Molly cocked her head, stretching her legs out in front of her and thinking hard as she gently tapped one foot against the ground and then the other to test what stage her pins and needles had got to. All she got in return was a mild tingle.

'Actually.... I think Olive's probably the best person to speak to. I mean... she's basically in charge of anything important on the island anyway,' said Molly. 'She'll know what to do - and what's best for everyone.'

'Okay, sounds like a plan,' said Tim. 'Are you ready to move?'

Molly nodded and before she knew what was happening, Tim was on his feet and reaching down to pull her up. Well... she wasn't going to turn down the chance to hold his lovely warm hands again, was she?!

'Cheers, she said, suddenly shy as she found herself just a couple of inches away from his face.

'My pleasure,' said Tim, leaning forward and kissing the end of her nose. 'Oh goodness, even that's cold!'

'Well don't go rubbing it!' chuckled Molly.

'Spoilsport!' breathed Tim, leaning in and pulling her into a deliciously warm kiss that made her toes curl.

'Shall we head to the Tallyaff now then?' said Molly, when Tim pulled away, leaving her feeling like she was floating.

'As much as I'd love to,' said Tim, 'I think we might have to leave that until later… or maybe even tomorrow.'

'Aw!' said Molly, sticking her bottom lip out.

Tim grinned at her and ran his thumb over the pouting lip. Molly instantly felt like her legs were in serious danger of giving out beneath her.

'I think I'd better do some more on this report while I'm here - just to keep the professor happy and off the scent. Then I can give him an update this evening with a clear conscience.'

'Okay,' sighed Molly.

'You gonna head back or help?' said Tim.

'Help?' she said. 'What does that involve?'

'Mainly wandering along, holding my hand and occasionally giving me a cuddle to warm up?' said Tim, shooting her a cheeky wink.

'Help!' said Molly promptly. 'Definitely help!'

CHAPTER 22

TIM

The following morning, it proved far easier for Tim to escape the rest of the group than he'd been expecting. He was about to enter the Dining Hall when he bumped into Rosie… who was looking a bit like she was at death's door.

'I'm going back to bed,' she mumbled, glancing at him with bleary eyes.

'Oh!' he said, taking a step back. 'What's up?'

'Sore throat… high temperature,' she snuffled, heading for the door. 'Just like everyone else.'

It took Tim all of five seconds before he had a fully formed escape plan. He'd jump on the bandwagon and feign the flu!

Letting himself into the Dining Hall, he spotted the professor at the far end of the room and made a beeline straight for him - doing his best to look as pathetic as humanly possible while he was at it. As soon as he drew close, Tim started to cough.

'I wanted to bring this down for you,' he spluttered, holding out his updated report.

Tim had to bite his lip as the professor took the pages from him, gripping them gingerly between his thumb and forefinger and looking at them as though they might be the source of the plague.

'I appreciate your diligence, Mr Stewart!' he said, his own voice coming out in an unhealthy-sounding wheeze. 'But it's back to bed for you, I think. You look dreadful. I'll be doing exactly the same as soon as I've got some honey and lemon. I'm not well enough to go out there today – and *you* certainly can't be trusted on the site without supervision!'

Tim just nodded. He had to resist the urge to lay it on a bit thicker by telling the professor how disappointed he was – but this wasn't his first rodeo. He'd learned as a kid that less was more when it came to playing hooky from school!

Continuing to look as feeble as possible, Tim backed away towards the door that led to the reception. Of course - the minute he was he was out of sight - he straightened up and grinned in triumph. With a decided bounce to his step, he ignored the door that led back up to his tower bedroom and let himself outside instead.

With a quick glance around to check that the coast was clear, Tim snuck around the back of the castle and headed for the spot where Molly promised she'd be waiting.

Sure enough, as he ducked under a wide stone archway, Tim spotted her little silver car. Molly already had the engine running, and he jumped in without daring to look over his shoulder.

'Go! Go! Go!' Tim yelled as he pulled his seatbelt on. Molly put her foot down with a giggle.

'Morning, by the way!' he chuckled.

'Morning,' she said with a grin, 'and what a beautiful one!'

She was right. With all the rushing around, Tim hadn't stopped to notice - but sure enough, the sky was a clear blue and there was very little wind.

'Did you get away okay?' said Molly, easing down the driveway and then putting her foot down again the minute she hit the main road.

'No problem!' said Tim. 'I think the professor thought my lurgy sounded worse than his.'

'What lurgy?' she said, shooting him a look. 'Do I need to start chugging down vitamin C?'

'Nah! Not on my account,' said Tim. 'Mine's completely fictitious… but I figured it was a convenient bandwagon to jump on, considering the rest of them seem to be hovering at death's door!'

'Yeah right!' tutted Molly. 'I think most of them just wanted a day off!'

'Fair enough!' said Tim.

'Anyway,' said Molly, 'it gave me the perfect excuse

to disappear for a bit. The professor wanted some cold and flu remedy, so I offered to go and buy him some from the Tallyaff.'

'Cunning!' said Tim.

'As a fox!' laughed Molly. 'Anyway, do you have the gold on you?'

'Of course!' said Tim, patting his pocket. 'As if I'd forget that!'

'Sorry,' said Molly, 'force of habit! Joyce is such a scatterbrain she forgets anything and everything. Honestly, I've lost track of the number of times I've gone down to meet the ferry – only to discover she's sent me there a day or even a week early.'

'Sounds like a nightmare!' said Tim. 'At least you had plenty of warning about us lot turning up – the university must have booked us in months ago.'

'Yeah… that would have been great - in theory,' sighed Molly.

'In theory?' said Tim.

'Joyce lost our bookings diary months ago,' she said. 'I got a forty-five-minute warning that you lot were turning up!'

'No wonder you looked a bit harassed!' laughed Tim. 'Aren't you ever tempted to leave?'

'Tempted?' echoed Molly. 'Every single day. But *you* try finding another full-time job on an island this small!'

'I can imagine,' said Tim. 'But… it must be a nightmare doing something that makes you so frustrated.'

'That's a bit rich coming from you,' she chuckled, 'considering you told me you're on a course you don't want to be on. Tempted to leave?'

'Touché!' said Tim, shaking his head. 'Yeah... of course I'm tempted. If it wasn't for mum, I'd have probably already done it! But hey - it's not all bad. I got to meet you, didn't I?'

'That is a very good point!' said Molly, shooting him a grin.

'Anyway... I think I really *would* drop out if I had a very good reason to... but...'

Tim promptly shut his mouth. He was pretty sure that Molly might end up being "a very good reason" - but they'd only just met. Now was *not* the time to start saying things like that out loud. For one thing, Molly was driving - and he had a feeling it might not be safe!

He *could* ask her to pull over, of course...

'Does Olive know we're coming?' he said lightly.

'Yep - I called ahead!' said Molly.

Nope - now was definitely not the time!

CHAPTER 23

MOLLY

Olive led the pair of them straight through into the pristine, empty kitchen of the Tallyaff... but she didn't stop there. Throwing open another door, she ushered them into a large, walk-in storeroom and then promptly closed the door behind the three of them.

'Is this really necessary?' laughed Molly, shooting a slightly apologetic look at Tim who had his eyebrows raised his eyebrows in amusement.

'You said we needed to talk without being disturbed,' said Olive with a little shrug. 'I mean, Mr Harris has already been in for his espresso, but you never know who else might turn up.'

'How *is* Mr Harris?' said Molly. 'Has he got over the trespassers yet?'

'Hardly! We had a long chat about how you lot are making a mess of the spot McGregor likes to do his business!' said Olive, turning to Tim. 'According to him, you've been scratching around with trowels right where he likes to go, and the poor lad's got constipation – he's having trouble choosing a new spot!'

Tim snorted.

'To be fair,' chuckled Molly, 'Tim's not the one who's been playing with trowels. He's been off checking other things out.'

'Other things?' said Olive, casting a sly look from Molly to Tim and then back again.

Molly felt her cheeks start to glow. She'd dearly love to give Olive a good prod - if only there was any way she could do it without Tim seeing.

'Yeah!' said Tim, jumping to her rescue. 'The prof decided to get rid of me by sending me off on a wild goose chase down by the stream.'

'Did he now?' laughed Olive. 'Find anything good?'

'A fish paste pot!' said Molly, nodding excitedly.

'Blimey - if that's what you've come to show me, we could have done this out in the bar!' laughed Olive. 'And if you think those old things are special, I can show you the spot locals have been dumping their rubbish in for centuries. I'm sure you'd find plenty more there!'

Molly watched Tim's eyes widen with excitement and she had to swallow a laugh. He looked almost as excited by that prospect as he did about the gold.

'I might take you up on that,' said Tim. 'But that's not what we wanted to talk to you about.

'Oh!' said Olive. 'Well - that's good, otherwise I'd think you'd need your head feeling.'

'It's this!' said Molly, unable to contain her excitement any longer. 'Show her, Tim!'

Tim nodded and, reaching into his pocket, drew out the crumpled blue napkin from her previous day's pastry.

Molly held her breath as he unfolded it carefully to show Olive the little pile of golden grains nestling in its crease. She kept her eyes on Olive the entire time - but her friend's face remained completely expressionless.

'Where did you find these?' she said at last.

'Upper Crum woods!' laughed Tim. 'Oops… not *quite* the right island!'

'He means the Wee Burn,' said Molly.

Olive stared at the little pile of gold for a long moment and then turned her gaze on Molly.

'And… *how* did you find it?' she asked.

'He… we… panned for it!' said Molly. 'Tim showed me how - with that wok he bought from you yesterday!'

Olive's stern expression dissolved into a laugh, and she shook her head in amusement.

'Well, at least that clears up that particular mystery!' she hooted. 'I have to admit, I was wondering what you were up to when you picked up that old thing while the others were all busy buying waterproofs.'

'You… erm… you don't seem that surprised about the gold,' said Tim, raising a curious eyebrow.

Olive shrugged. 'I *am* surprised you found some… but only because I thought it had all been found already.'

'Wait - you knew about it?' said Molly in surprise.

'Of course,' said Olive. 'I mean, where do you think they found the money to build the castle in the first place? I honestly thought it was dug up centuries ago.'

'But… we found some!' said Tim, blinking in surprise.

'First bits I've seen in ages, to be honest,' said Olive with a shrug. 'A couple of tiny pieces turned up back in the 1950s - but the people who found it were tourists. They just assumed it was fool's gold. You know that… that…?!' she clicked her fingers several times, clearly looking for the right word.

'Iron pyrites?' prompted Tim.

'That. Exactly!' said Olive, pointing at him.

'But it wasn't, was it?' he said. 'I mean… this isn't…' he added, nodding down to the precious grains the pair of them had found.

'Nope, it wasn't,' agreed Olive. 'Just like this isn't. I should imagine that's pure Crumcarey gold you've got there, alright!'

'What happened to the stuff from the 50s?' said Molly curiously.

'Oh, it got handed in at the shop,' said Olive. 'That was before my time, of course, but I think I've still got it around here somewhere. My hubby put it into one of those old plastic tubs camera film used to come in - you know the ones?'

Tim nodded. 'But... you just kept it? And no one's thought to go searching for more?'

'We just kept it,' said Olive, eyeballing him.

Molly noticed that that her friend was now giving Tim a shrewd look - as if she was trying to figure out if she could trust him or not.

'Here's the thing,' said Olive, lowering her voice and leaning in, so that they were in a sort of three-person huddle, 'it wasn't worth much - even with the price of gold these days. Besides – everyone on the island knows. It's kind of a poorly kept secret around here.'

'But I've never heard of it before,' said Molly. 'And why's it a secret anyway?'

'Well... maybe it's a secret we've kept better than we realise, then!' amended Olive. 'Why it's a secret is easy, though. We've always kept it quiet because we simply don't want to attract too much of the wrong kind of attention.'

Molly glanced at Tim. He was nodding slowly, clearly letting it all sink in. Suddenly, she had a feeling they were lucky to be dealing with another islander. Not only was Tim a great guy - but he also understood what it was like to live on a tiny island and how the community pulled together and protected itself.

'Imagine if everyone knew,' said Olive, her voice now deadly serious. 'Imagine if it ever got out. Crumcarey would be trampled by people looking for gold.

We'd be overrun with tourists with pans and metal detectors… and that's if we look on the bright side. If a large, commercial outfit got it into their heads to really look into it - it could spell disaster.'

'I get it,' said Tim quietly. Molly noticed that he was looking a little bit sick. 'I'd hate for something like that to happen on Brumeldsay… so yeah…'

'But… what do we do?' said Molly, feeling weirdly deflated, as though someone had just stuck a pin in her and she'd got a slow puncture.

'It depends,' said Olive. 'Who exactly have you told about this already? Joyce?'

Olive's face had taken on a slightly fierce look, and Molly took a surreptitious step backwards. She knew that Olive and Joyce didn't see eye to eye at the best of times. Joyce wasn't exactly *good* for Crumcarey. Her grotty cabins and half-arsed attempts at running her business didn't give the island a good name – and that was something Olive took very seriously.

'I promise - we haven't told Joyce,' said Molly, shaking her head and holding her hands up in surrender.

'Good,' said Olive, sagging with relief. 'Because… if she knew about the gold, there would be no telling what she'd do!'

'We came to you first,' said Tim.

'And will you be telling that professor of yours?' countered Olive.

Tim shook his head. 'Definitely not.'

'Good. Right… well, I think for now the best thing might be if you hang up that wok of yours,' she said, shooting him a wink. 'Before anyone figures out what you're up to!'

'And… that's it?' said Molly.

'And that's it,' said Olive kindly - but with a sense of finality that brooked no argument - from either of them.

'Okay,' said Tim, with an easy shrug. 'Sounds like a good plan from where I'm standing!'

CHAPTER 24

TIM

The little car was definitely a lot quieter as they pulled away from the Tallyaff. The playful banter was missing, and in its place was a kind of stunned silence. Their great discovery hadn't actually turned out to be a discovery at all.

'Disappointed?' said Tim gently, turning to look at Molly. She was focusing intently on the road ahead, and there was a little crease on her forehead again.

'Not really!' she said after a bit of a pause. 'I was just thinking… the fun part about the whole thing was finding the gold in the first place!'

'Woman after my own heart!' said Tim with a smile. 'Anyway - how were we to know that practically everyone on the island already knows about it!'

'Other than Joyce,' laughed Molly.

Tim nodded, glad that the strange tension seemed to be lifting.

'I mean... it was wonderful that we got to find it together,' said Molly. 'It's something I'll never forget.'

She paused, and Tim saw her swallow hard as if there was something she wanted to say but for some reason, she'd stopped herself.

'Anyway,' she continued, shaking her head slightly, 'I wouldn't want to make a fuss about it. Imagine... if it went wrong... it's like Olive said - it could ruin Crumcarey forever!'

'Yeah,' said Tim. 'She's definitely right. Besides... I found something way more valuable than the gold!'

'You didn't tell me that!' said Molly indignantly. 'What? What did you find?'

'You!' he said simply.

Molly opened her mouth to reply, but the words didn't seem to want to come out. Tim watched her in amusement for a couple of seconds before taking pity on her.

'Who'd have thought that being on the wrong course would lead me to the wrong standing stones on the wrong island... but I'd meet the *right* person.'

'The right person?' Molly echoed quietly.

'The right person,' he said again. 'I mean... I don't know how it would work if...'

Tim paused, not quite sure if it was such a good idea to be saying this out loud.

Was he talking nonsense here?

Was it just him feeling this way?

Sure, they'd kissed and kissed... and then kissed

some. He'd *hoped* Molly might be feeling the same - excited about what might happen next...

What if he was wrong?

Crumcarey was Molly's home - but he'd be gone in just a few days. Tim had no idea where his future might lead him. He wasn't sure if he'd finish his course... or move back to Brumeldsay... or go off on some other adventure instead. But somehow, he knew his future wasn't here on Crumcarey.

'If *what* exactly?' said Molly, pulling into a passing place and killing the engine.

'I... we... if...' Tim spluttered as she turned to him.

'If we see where this goes?' said Molly quietly, lifting an eyebrow.

'Well, yeah!' said Tim.

'I know exactly where you and I are going,' said Molly.

'You... you do?' he said in surprise.

'Sure I do. Just over there!' she pointed down towards the sea. As Tim followed her gaze, he spotted the old ice cream van parked up between the dunes. 'We're going for an ice cream!' she added with a grin.

'That wasn't *quite* what I meant,' laughed Tim.

'After we've had an ice cream, we're going to sneak back into the castle and we're going up to your room,' she said, catching his eye and holding it.

Tim swallowed nervously. There was a glint there that told him his hunch about her was right - Molly Mackenzie definitely spelled trouble.

'Why?' he said. 'To hide the gold?'

'Well,' said Molly, 'a little birdie told me you're *very* poorly - so I'm going to tuck you up nice and cosy… and then, if you're very lucky, I might just show you that tattoo!'

Tim laughed out loud as he watched Molly open the car door and clamber out.

'Come on, Mr To Be Confirmed!' she called, beckoning for him to follow. 'I want that ice cream. Every big, important decision in life is easier if you've got ice cream dripping down your chin.'

'I like your style,' whispered Tim, before climbing out of the car and following Molly down towards the beach.

CHAPTER 25

MOLLY

Four months later...

Sea spray drifted on the breeze, coating Molly's face with fine droplets of salt water. It was so very familiar... and yet, this was all completely new too.

Molly was on a ferry... but this wasn't the boat to Crumcarey. This one was bigger - though it was just as decrepit and battered as the one she knew and loved. In the distance, she could just make out a golden shore - and behind it, the tell-tale signs of an ancient forest.

'Brumeldsay!' sighed Tim from his vantage point next to her. 'Nearly home!'

'Looks just like Crumcarey to me!' said Molly, earning herself a dig in the ribs. 'Oi!' she chuckled. 'I just meant it looks a lot like the guidebook!'

Tim grinned at her, and Molly felt her heart flip - just like every single time he'd smiled at her over the four months since they'd first met. Now - at long last – they were on their way to Brumeldsay. Molly couldn't wait to meet Tim's mum and explore the island she'd heard so much about.

'Are you looking forward to seeing the house?' said Tim, dropping a kiss on her forehead before turning back to stare at his island home as they sailed ever nearer.

'Are you kidding me?!' she laughed. 'I can't wait!'

After his first visit to Crumcarey, Tim had returned to the mainland with the others. He'd stuck with the course for as long as he could stand… which turned out to be not that long at all. As soon as the professor submitted paperwork to start the process of getting Crumcarey's standing stones registered as an ancient monument - he decided to call it quits.

It had been funny to begin with - but the entire charade seemed to be building up a head of steam, and Tim hadn't wanted to have any part of it. Joyce had been overjoyed by the development, of course. It would mean plenty more visitors to the island… and she had no qualms about charging them through the nose to stay in the grotty portacabins. Of course, if it had been up to Molly, she'd have done everything in her power to push forward with renovating more rooms in the castle. Joyce wasn't having any of it.

That wasn't Molly's issue to deal with anymore

though… because the minute Tim quit his course, she'd handed in her notice. Neither of them knew where life would take them in the end – but they'd decided wherever it was, they'd go there together.

'Excited?' whispered Tim.

'You have no idea!' she chuckled.

Molly wasn't sure she'd *ever* been this excited in her life. In fact, she couldn't quite believe this was really happening. She was moving to Brumeldsay with this gorgeous man. Neither of them knew how long they'd stay, but for now, that didn't matter – they were on their way to their first home together.

Shivering slightly and swallowing down a wave of pure joy, Molly snuggled into Tim's side.

'Oh - I nearly forgot,' said Tim, nuzzling her hair and making her squirm.

'Forgot what?' said Molly.

'I've got a little surprise for you.'

'Oh yeah?' she said, raising an eyebrow and noticing that Tim's dimples had come out to play.

'Yeah,' said Tim, looking more than a little bit pleased with himself. 'Moll… I'm not sure about much at the moment - but I *am* sure about one thing.'

'What's that?' said Molly, turning to look at him properly.

'You,' he said simply.

'Soppy git!' she said with a grin. 'Nice surprise though, thanks!'

'You haven't seen it yet!' laughed Tim, reaching into his jacket pocket.

'Oh?' said Molly. 'Oh!' she said again, eyeballing the little black octagonal box that was now sitting in the palm of his hand.

'I spoke to everyone back on Crumcarey,' said Tim quietly. 'When they realised we were serious... that *I* was serious... they all had a good rummage around.'

'I... I don't understand,' said Molly.

'I spoke to Olive,' said Tim, 'and it turned out she had a bit more gold tucked away than she realised. And somehow, Mr Harris heard about it too and gave me a nugget the size of a pea... and... well...'

Tim paused and flipped open the little box. It was full to the brim with grains of Crumcarey gold.

'Olive thinks there's enough in here for a ring,' said Tim.

'Oh... she does, does she?' said Molly. 'Well... it's like I said before, Olive's usually right.'

'Only if you're interested, of course?' said Tim.

The sound of the waves and the distant calls of the patrolling gulls receded as she stared at the contents of the little box - a precious reminder of where she'd come from – her past.

Molly looked up into Tim's eyes and smiled.

This was her future. This man, right here - with his easy smile and dimples that made her go weak at the knees. This kindred spirit who'd wandered onto her island by accident and swept her off her feet.

'So,' said Tim, 'what do you think?'
'I think it sounds like an adventure,' she said.

THE END

ALSO BY BETH RAIN

Standalone Books:

How to be Angry at Christmas

Little Bamton Series:

Little Bamton: The Complete Series Collection: Books 1 - 5

Individual titles:

Christmas Lights and Snowball Fights (Little Bamton Book 1)

Spring Flowers and April Showers (Little Bamton Book 2)

Summer Nights and Pillow Fights (Little Bamton Book 3)

Autumn Cuddles and Muddy Puddles (Little Bamton Book 4)

Christmas Flings and Wedding Rings (Little Bamton Book 5)

Upper Bamton Series:

Upper Bamton: The Complete Series Collection: Books 1 - 4

Upper Bamton Series:

A New Arrival in Upper Bamton (Upper Bamton Book 1)

Rainy Days in Upper Bamton (Upper Bamton Book 2)

Hidden Treasures in Upper Bamton (Upper Bamton Book 3)

Time Flies By in Upper Bamton (Upper Bamton Book 4)

Crumcarey Island Series:

Christmas on Crumcarey (Crumcarey Island Book 1)

All Change on Crumcarey (Crumcarey Island Book 2)

Making Waves on Crumcarey (Crumcarey Island Book 3)

Fool's Gold on Crumcarey (Crumcarey Island Book 4)

Seabury Series:

Welcome to Seabury (Seabury Book 1)

Trouble in Seabury (Seabury Book 2)

Christmas in Seabury (Seabury Book 3)

Sandwiches in Seabury (Seabury Book 4)

Secrets in Seabury (Seabury Book 5)

Surprises in Seabury (Seabury Book 6)

Dreams and Ice Creams in Seabury (Seabury Book 7)

Mistakes and Heartbreaks in Seabury (Seabury Book 8)

Laughter and Happy Ever After in Seabury (Seabury Book 9)

A Quiet Life in Seabury (Seabury Book 10)

In A Spin in Seabury (Seabury Book 11)

Living The Dream in Seabury (Seabury Book 12)

Seabury Series Collections:

Kate's Story: Books 1 - 3

Hattie's Story: Books 4 - 6

Standalones: Books 7 - 9

Lizzie's Story: Books 10 - 12

Writing as Bea Fox:

What's a Girl To Do? The Complete Series

Individual titles:

The Holiday: What's a Girl To Do? (Book 1)

The Wedding: What's a Girl To Do? (Book 2)

The Lookalike: What's a Girl To Do? (Book 3)

The Reunion: What's a Girl To Do? (Book 4)

At Christmas: What's a Girl To Do? (Book 5)

ABOUT THE AUTHOR

Beth Rain has always wanted to be a writer and has been penning adventures for characters ever since she learned to stare into the middle-distance and daydream.

She recently moved to a windswept, Scottish island, and it is a dream come true to spend her days hanging out with Bob – her trusty laptop – scoffing crisps and chocolate while dreaming up swoony love stories for all her imaginary friends.

Beth's writing will always deliver on the happy-ever-afters, so if you need cosy… you're in safe hands!

Visit www.bethrain.com for all the bookish goodness and keep up with all Beth's news by joining her monthly newsletter!

facebook.com/BethRainBooks
twitter.com/bethrainauthor
instagram.com/bethrainauthor

Printed in Great Britain
by Amazon